NEVE

Alan Scholefield was originally a journa̶l̶i̶s̶t̶ ̶...̶ ̶...̶ ̶...̶ he
novelist in the early sixties. He is now the author of more than twenty
novels, one of which, *Venom*, was filmed starring Nicol Williamson,
Sarah Miles, and Oliver Reed. He has also written screen plays, a stage
adaptation of *Treasure Island*, and two thirteen-part adventure series for
TV, as well as five suspense novels under the pseudonym of Lee Jordan.
He is married to the novelist Anthea Goddard and has three daughters.

Never Die in January

Alan Scholefield

CRIME

PAN BOOKS
IN ASSOCIATION WITH MACMILLAN LONDON

First published 1992 by Macmillan London Limited

This edition published 1993 by Pan Books Limited
a division of Pan Macmillan Publishers Limited
Cavaye Place London SW10 9PG
and Basingstoke

in association with Macmillan London Limited

Associated companies throughout the world

ISBN 0 330 32854 9

1 3 5 7 9 8 6 4 2

A CIP catalogue record for this book is available from
the British Library

Phototypeset by Intype, London
Printed and bound in Great Britain by
BPCC Paperbacks Ltd
Member of BPCC Ltd

FOR RONNIE AND BRIAN BROWN

ACKNOWLEDGEMENT

My thanks for his help go to Detective Inspector Hugh Toomer of the Metropolitan Police (Retd.). Any mistakes are my own.

1

Knives.

What sort of knives?

Kitchen knives.

What sort of kitchen knives: filleting? paring? cutting? slicing? chopping?

He was patronizing her. She knew that.

And they were talking too much.

She had seen the old-fashioned ironmonger's shop as she drove into the village a few minutes earlier. She had been looking for a place like it and there it was in the January fog, its windows stuffed with things she had never seen before and some she had never thought to see again: who used a hand-mincer these days?

The place smelled of creosote and Stockholm tar. The man behind the counter – an old-fashioned long wooden counter backed by scores of small labelled drawers – was elderly and thin and wore a long brown shop coat.

He stood waiting, not hiding his impatience.

Didn't he have a general purpose kind of knife?

She shouldn't be talking like this. In and out. That's what she had planned. But if she left abruptly he might consider her rude and remember her.

A general-purpose knife? He didn't know about that.

His voice had changed and so had his manner. It was no longer patronizing. For a moment, caught by her hot eyes, he seemed unsure of himself.

He brought out three knives. They looked alike: shining blades, needle points, black wooden handles, brass rivets.

French.

He shouldn't say it but they were the best. Carbon steel. People

7

didn't like it much these days because it stained. But there was nothing to touch it for taking an edge.

She wanted to stop him there. To get out. To become anonymous. But he'd remember her then. She let him talk.

The smallest of the three. Vegetable knife. For paring, boning, that sort of thing. He put it down.

Filleting knife. Whippy. Slice anything with that.

The third. Cook's knife. Heavier than the others. Six-inch blade. Chopping. Cutting. Most things. General purpose, hadn't she said? She could peel an apple – or kill a pig with this if she'd a mind to.

She paid cash, went back to her car, and drove through the fog.

She came to a town. No more ironmongers, no more little scenes that could be remembered.

This time the kitchen department of a chain store. A bored young salesman.

She asked to see some knives.

Kitchen knives.

Of carbon steel.

2

'Never die in January, laddie,' Macrae said to Silver. 'It's a bloody awful month.'

They were burying Eddie Twyford south of the river in one of those bleak cemeteries that spread for miles along the Southern Railway: a landscape of marble, dead flowers, and bones.

Silver was momentarily startled, for Macrae's voice was loud enough for everyone at the grave side to hear.

Everyone was six.

There was the priest, the two men from the undertakers, Macrae, Silver – and the widow, Gladys.

The priest, his surplice blowing up over his shoulders as the bitter east wind cut across the open spaces, looked sharply round at Macrae. He didn't want interruptions, didn't want anything to go wrong, he wanted the coffin in the ground, the earth on top of it, a last fast prayer for the quick and the dead, then hot soup in the presbytery.

'Six people,' Macrae said. 'Not much for a life.'

There was bitterness and anger in his voice and Silver knew why. He himself should have been feeling much the same but wasn't. Macrae might have known it would come to . . . well, not quite to this, but to *something* unpleasant.

It was a day Dickens would have recognized. There was fog on the river and fog in the streets; fog amongst the gravestones and in the branches of the trees. Fog everywhere.

Macrae hunched down in his long dark overcoat and said, 'You ever read *Bleak House* at your university?' He always managed to invest the phrase with irony, as though pretending to believe Silver's education was a myth.

9

Silver saw the priest turn crossly from his book again and instead of replying shook his head.

He turned away from Macrae so that he would not be receptive to more questions. The two detectives were a contrast in shapes and styles. Macrae was big, burly, dressed in a long overcoat and holding an old-fashioned brown trilby; Silver was dark, also bareheaded, wearing black not because of the funeral but because he fancied himself in black and wore it most of the time. Where Macrae had a broad, heavy face and head that was often lowered like a bull's, Silver's face was thin and angular, his eyes sharply intelligent, and his black hair sat closely on his skull. Macrae looked exactly what he was, a Metropolitan policeman. Silver did not.

He looked across the open grave to Gladys Twyford. She was elderly and square and was wearing a black coat and black hat. Her face had congealed in the cold and it wore a puzzled expression as though she could not understand what was going on and that in a few moments Eddie would appear with the car and drive them off to the nearest pub for a drink.

Eddie had *always* been behind the wheels of cars. He'd been Macrae's driver for years, even after drivers had been banned – as part of a cost-cutting exercise – for middle-ranking detectives.

And that had been the problem. That's what had killed him.

'We therefore commit his body to the ground; earth to earth . . . '

But the earth, the mound of soil which perched at the grave side, had been dug the day before and was frozen hard. The trowel gave a mournful clang as the priest tried to dig into it. One of the undertaker's men kicked the surface and broke off several lumps. He placed them in the trowel and the priest sprinkled them on to the coffin. It sounded like machine-gun fire.

' . . . ashes to ashes, dust to dust; in sure and certain hope of the Resurrection to eternal life . . . '

Crack . . . crack . . . crack . . .

The hard lumps of earth cascaded down as Gladys Twyford, her hand trembling, took the trowel for the last time.

A moment's prayer from the priest, handshakes all round, a lingering one for Gladys, and then he was off down the concrete pathway, cassock billowing, hair blowing . . . Soup was beckoning.

The undertakers put their hats back on their heads and folded up the coffin straps. A grave digger who had been watching with impatience in the lee of a tall gravestone hurried forward with pickaxe and shovel to entomb the coffin. Eddie Twyford, policeman, driver, and latterly records clerk in Scotland Yard, had departed this life.

Silver took Macrae and Gladys in his Golf. She had asked them to come back for a drink and something to eat. Neither man wanted to, neither had been able to find an excuse. They drove towards the estate in Lambeth where she lived.

'He could have been cremated,' she said. 'But he wouldn't have it. Wanted a proper funeral. He's been paying for that grave for years and years. Since ever I first knew him. Didn't matter how skint, he'd rather put two bob into the burial fund than have a second pint.'

She paused. 'I wonder if he'd have liked it. The funeral, I mean. He was always a person for getting what he was paying for. Picked out his own coffin. There was a special offer once. Wouldn't have it. Wanted his made of wood not plastic, with proper brass handles. I said, Eddie, what's it matter? You ain't going to be there to see it . . . But he wouldn't have it otherwise . . . '

The traffic was heavy and they took nearly forty minutes to reach the Green Leas Estate. Gladys talked all the way.

'It's not actually green, is it?' Macrae said softly. He was sitting in front with Silver – not even funerals could cause him to force his bulk into the rear of small cars. 'The only green thing about it is the drawings.'

Most of the apartment-block walls had been aerosoled. Apart from a jumble of names . . . of who had been there and when . . . there were several 'paintings' done mostly in greens and purples and reds.

The estate was huge. Ranks of buildings, all the same shape and height, disappeared into the foggy distance. In a sandpit, meant for kids to play in but long since abandoned, lay an upturned pram and an old iron-framed bed. The mattress had been slit open and coir was blowing in the wind. Derelict wheel-less cars were dotted about what had once been a green lea with genuine green grass and trees with real organic leaves. Now everything looked like a stage-set for a posthumous play by Beckett.

'I'd write my name on a wall if I lived here,' Silver said. 'At least I'd know I'd existed.'

'Famous for fifteen seconds? Don't be bloody sentimental.'

Just then out of the mist a group of youths crossed the road ahead of them.

'That's them!' Gladys said.

'Who?' Macrae turned to her.

'The yobs that done for Eddie.'

'Eddie died of a heart attack, Mrs Twyford,' Silver said. Already lies were being piled on lies.

'Well, you know what I mean. If it hadn't been for them—'

'And Scales,' Macrae said. 'Don't forget Kenneth bloody Scales.'

Silver slowed down. The youths stopped and turned to look at the car. There were eight or nine of them aged between fourteen and eighteen. They turned as though on cue and there was some-thing deeply menacing about it, Silver thought.

'You want me to stop, guv'nor?' he said.

Macrae shook his head. 'No, drive on.'

Silver was relieved. It would have been just like Macrae . . . No, that wasn't true. You didn't get to be a Detective Superintendent for doing stupid things. Macrae knew his business best. Silver often had to tell himself this when it seemed, as in the case of Eddie Twyford, that Macrae was being unnecessarily obtuse. He was blaming Scales, the deputy commander at Cannon Row police station, for Eddie's death. Gladys was blaming the yobbos. But, in Silver's opinion, if anyone was to blame it was Macrae.

They parked the car directly outside Gladys's sitting-room win-dows on the ground floor and Silver hurried into the flat so that he would not be out of sight of the vehicle for more than a few seconds. A couple of minutes and the stereo would go. A couple more and there wouldn't be a wheel left.

The year before, Silver and his girl Zoe had gone on holiday

12

to Namibia, in south-west Africa, to look at wildlife. In one of the huge game parks in that hot and sandy country they had come across the newly killed carcass of a wildebeest on which three lions were feeding. They stopped the car and sat watching. When the lions finished it was the turn of hyenas, jackals, bat-eared foxes, vultures, marabou storks, and crows. The following morning the carcass was simply a collection of whitening bones.

Silver hadn't thought about the incident since then. In the Green Leas Estate it came easily to mind; the metaphor was obvious.

Gladys said, 'Now Mr Macrae, I know you like a drop of whisky, you being a Scotchman. And Sergeant Silver? Eddie had some bottles of lager—'

'Whisky will be fine, Mrs Twyford.'

'It's no trouble. He always kept a bottle or two in the cupboard . . . '

She went out to the kitchen.

'I wonder where all the plants went,' Macrae said. 'It used to be a jungle in here.'

Silver stood by the window keeping an eye on the car.

'We were wondering about the plants,' Macrae said when Gladys returned. She was carrying a tray with bottles.

'Eddie threw them out,' she said. 'Years it took to grow them like they was. Then one day he throws them out. Says he must have a clear field.'

'For what?' Silver was puzzled.

'Them.' She indicated the outdoors with her thumb. 'In case they ever got inside.'

'Oh.' Silver assumed she meant the youths they had seen.

She took doilies off two plates of sandwiches and a dish of sausage rolls. 'Egg? Potted meat?'

They each took two.

'Would you like me to heat up the sausage rolls?'

'No, no,' Macrae said. 'They're just fine.'

'I should have cooked something. A man needs a hot meal. Eddie always . . . he always . . . ' She began to cry, not loudly, just a soft snivelling. 'I'm sorry . . . I'll be all right in a moment . . . '

'Let it all out,' Macrae said.

13

'It's just that I . . . you know it was so sudden. That's why . . . I mean three days ago he was here, right in this sitting-room . . . and now . . . '

She had opened a window on a bleak and lonely future.

'Mr Macrae, I'm frightened. They won't leave off now that Eddie's gone. You'll see. It'll be worse. Can't you do something?'

'I just wish I could. But you've got to catch them red-handed and—'

'But couldn't you talk to them? Eddie always said, "Mr Macrae'll talk to them. He'll fix it."'

Silver thought of the patrol of youths they had just seen. That's what they seemed like to him: a patrol. A group patrolling without organization but with a shared desire to find something – anything – to relieve their boredom.

'What about moving to another part of London?' Silver said.

'We asked the housing. We applied. They said there were waiting lists. It's no use. When Eddie was here, well . . . we had each other. But now . . . '

'They may not worry you again,' Macrae said. 'They had it in for Eddie because he'd been in the police. But they've nothing against you.'

She looked unconvinced. 'You know what they did? I don't even like to mention it. But they . . . they pushed a parcel through the letter box. Wrapped newspapers. And inside the newspapers . . . '

Her chin began to tremble and tears came to her eyes again. 'I can't say it. I just can't. Nobody does things like that. I mean I never even heard of such a thing before . . . But they did it.' She paused. Macrae chomped on his sausage roll. 'I'm not young any more,' she said. 'I can't go on like this. Mr Macrae, why is it that it's the elderly that suffer? Why can't the government look after us better?'

'God knows, and that's the truth.'

They stayed another half an hour then went out into the cold afternoon.

Silver said, 'I don't like leaving her, guv'nor.'

'What the hell can we do about it?'

They drove slowly through the estate. A single youth was walking along the middle of the road with his back to them. Silver flashed his lights. The youth didn't take the slightest notice.

'Come on, come on,' Silver said.

'You sound just like Eddie. Hoot him.'

Silver tapped the hooter. The youth took no notice. 'Shit!' Macrae said. 'I've had enough of these bloody ego trips. Stop.'

Silver pulled up just ahead of the youth. He was about sixteen, short, burly, with cropped hair, a single earring in his nose, and tattoos on his hands. He wore tight-fitting jeans, Doc Marten boots, a long khaki parka, and a chain round his neck.

'Come here, sonny,' Macrae said. He stood massively in the middle of the road, his head thrust forward like a bull's.

'You talking to me?'

'That's right, sonny.'

Silver had turned the car side-on and had kept the engine running in case the 'patrol' suddenly came upon them. Near his hand was a large shifting-spanner. It lived by the driver's seat. His 'gun', Zoe called it.

The youth faltered. The aggression began to melt. He looked over his shoulder but he was alone. Macrae beckoned slowly with his finger.

'Why?' the youth said.

'Because I say so, sonny.'

'Who the hell are you?'

'I'm a policeman.'

His hand shot out and caught the youth by his scruffy T-shirt and pulled him closer. The other hand gripped his ear. The youth cried out.

'Listen to me, sonny, you and your mates are annoying me. You follow? And you're annoying people who live here, especially old people. You've been shoving nasty parcels through their letter boxes and making life a bloody misery for them . . . '

'You're hurting me!'

'Stand still then! So what I'm saying is stop it! OK? Otherwise I'll be back and I'll pull it right out by the roots. You understand? Say it!'

'Yeah. I understand.'

'On your way then!'

The youth walked off the road, stood under a tree and watched Macrae get back into the car. 'Bastards!' he said. But he said it softly.

Silver drove slowly across the river, on to the Embankment, and made for Cannon Row. Neither man spoke. It had been a rotten afternoon.

Gladys Twyford stood alone in the middle of her sitting-room. For some seconds she seemed unwilling to move, then, with a sigh, she began to clear up. She noticed that Silver had hardly touched his whisky. Most of the food was uneaten.

'What'll I do with it?' she said out loud. Since Eddie's death she found herself doing this more and more. It was as though she could not stand the silence of the empty flat. She wished she had something alive to talk to but they weren't allowed to keep pets on the Green Leas Estate. So she had begun to talk to a brown-and-white china bulldog which Eddie had brought home from a fair many years before. It sat on the fake mantelpiece – there was no fireplace – with its pink tongue hanging out. She had never liked it much, now it was her only companion.

'I'll put it in the fridge,' she said. 'Eat it later.'

When she'd cleared up she came back into the sitting room and stood looking out at the bleak urban landscape. Dusk was falling. She stood there for a few moments in the grey unlighted room, hidden by the curtains so that 'they' would not see her. Then she closed the curtains, put on the lights, and began the long and complicated task of preparing the flat, like some castle in old Outremer, against the besieging terrors of the night.

3

'But why?' Manfred Silver said for the umpteenth time. 'Why can't—'

'Why?' his wife repeated, shrilly. 'Because your daughter goes to hospital, that is why!'

'For a tooth!' He threw up his clean piano-teacher's hands in contempt. 'I never went to the hospital for a tooth.'

'Not a tooth. A wisdom tooth. An infected wisdom tooth.'

'You told me impacted.'

'Infected *and* impacted. They have to cut it out. So Ruth goes to hospital. I've explained all this a million times.'

Lottie Silver, in her sixties, wife of Manfred, once of Vienna, now of north-west London – the unfashionable part – made as though to go about her business, but Manfred, once Silberbauer, who only came from *near* Vienna, as Lottie often pointed out, blocked her path.

'But why—?'

'No! No more whys, no more buts. While Ruth is in hospital Stanley must go to kindergarten; Sidney must go to work (*vurk*). *Someone* must look after our grandson and our son-in-law.'

'And what (*vot*) about me?'

They had agreed, when first they had come to England, to speak the language of their adopted country to each other, but under the strain of the argument syntax and pronunciation were breaking down.

'That is why Zoe comes over. Zoe *and* Leo. They will look after you.'

Manfred pulled at his Vandyke beard, always a sign that he was agitated. 'But where will they sleep?'

'What?'

17

'There is only one spare room.'

'That's where they'll sleep. Where else?'

'But they're not married.'

Lottie stared at her husband in silence for a moment. She saw a short, portly man with a mass of grey hair. She herself had grey hair and it was untidy and her face was flushed from arguing. Slowly she shook her head in pity and amazement.

'Manfy . . . Manfy . . . What am I going to do with you? They have been living together for ages. They have a flat together.'

'In Pimlico,' Manfred said, as though Pimlico was Sodom. 'Not here.'

This exchange had taken place the day before. Now nemesis, in the shape of his son, Detective Sergeant Leopold Silver, and Leo's girl, Zoe Bertram, unmarried and not of this parish, was catching up with Manfred.

'Just remember,' Leo said to Zoe as they drove across London towards the old-fashioned apartment, 'wash your hands every ten minutes and dad will love you for ever and ever.'

'I know . . . ' Zoe said, with bravado, 'I've been before.'

But underneath that bravado there was a nervous substratum. She had accompanied Leo to occasional lunches and dinners but had never before stayed in the large old-fashioned mansion flat. The Silvers had always made her uneasy.

There was the cooking, for instance. 'Jewish food? Is that what he likes? Gefilte fish? Matzos balls? I can get them from Blooms.'

'Don't be silly. He's not some rare exotic species. Anyway, we never really eat Jewish, we eat, well, just what you and I eat.'

'Bacon? Ham? That sort of thing?'

'For Christ's sake, he won't be wearing a koppel. And he's not Hasidic, so he's not going to be wearing a black hat either. You know him, you've seen him before. Don't make such a big deal out of it.'

'Leo.'

'Yeah?'

'I want you to be with me. I don't want to have to entertain him in the evenings.'

'Of course.'

'And Leo.'

'Yeah?'

'Just remember, old buddy, like father like son. I'll be watching you.'

'Like mother, like daughter.'

'Being a vegetarian isn't illegal.'

'Your mother lives in that . . . that . . .'

'Co-operative. That's the word. The Alternative Technology Co-operative. And there's nothing illegal about that either.'

This was the kind of tension the Silver family managed to create, even *in absentia*.

The evening was not as bad as she had anticipated. Manfred had had his supper before they arrived – cold cuts left by Lottie. His habit, like that of great potentates, was to rise from the table when he had finished and leave the disposal of dishes, napkins, etc., to others. In this case it was Zoe, and she took his dishes into the kitchen and generally cleaned up while he played chess with Leo.

'How's Ruth?' Zoe said, to break the silence.

'Queen,' Manfred warned Leo. Leo moved his queen out of harm's way.

Zoe waited, but the subject of Ruth was not pursued. She picked up the paper, saw her reflection in a wall mirror and mouthed silently at herself, *She's fine, zank yew*.

At that moment Manfred looked up from the board and saw her apparently talking to herself. Hastily he turned away as though having surprised her in something despicable. He recovered and said, 'She's having a tooth out.'

Leo said, 'We know that, Dad, anyway it's not just a tooth it's a wisdom tooth.'

'A tooth is a tooth.'

Zoe sat on the sofa and read the paper until the game was over. Manfred won. There was a sharp exchange about Leo's missed opportunities and then Manfred stood up and said, 'I'm going to bed. Goodnight.' He paused at the door. 'Sleep where you like, I don't care.'

They heard him go into the bathroom. 'What did he mean by that?' Zoe said.

'God knows. Father's mind is impenetrable.'

They watched the late news and went to bed. The spare-room bed was icy.

19

'For God's sake!' Leo said, as she put her feet against his legs. 'They're freezing.'

' "Put them against me," you used to say. "I'll warm them up," you used to say. Things have certainly changed.'

'Give them to me. I'll rub them.'

The light was still on and he looked down at her as he rubbed her feet. She was small and dark and gypsy-looking, with wide-spaced brown eyes and high cheekbones.

She said, 'Is this what's called foreplay in the Metropolitan Police? Rubbing feet?'

'Sssh. Not so loud.'

'I just want to know your plans.'

He stopped, listening. She pulled his head down and kissed him. After a moment he drew away and listened again.

'What's the matter?'

'Nothing.'

'Yes there is.'

'It's . . . well . . . I don't think I can make it here. Not with my father—'

'But he's gone to bed.'

'Doesn't matter. It's not natural to me here. Listen!'

'What?'

'Can't you hear? He's in his music-room. He's pacing.'

'Leo, you're a basket-case. Lock the door if it bothers you.'

He locked the door and came back to bed but it didn't change anything. 'It's mental,' he said.

They lay next to each other under the bedclothes and held hands. 'Darby and Joan,' she said.

After a while he said, 'I went to Eddie Twyford's funeral this afternoon.'

He described the miserable group at the grave and said, 'Macrae started complaining about how few there were. And he was right. The priest didn't like it, though.' He paused for a few moments and said, 'Cremation for me.'

'Don't talk like that.'

'No, I mean it. When I go I don't want to be stuck in a box in one of those places.'

'Leo, don't. Not now.'

'Just as long as you know.'

20

'All right. I know!'

'I felt sorry for Gladys.'

'Gladys?'

'Eddie's widow. She seemed so . . . defenceless . . . They don't have any kids. So it's just her now. And she lives on this estate. That's another thing. I'm not living on an estate. Not ever.'

'Right. Cremation. No estates.'

'You should have seen it. You know those old black-and-white newsreels of World War I, Passchendaele and the Somme?'

'Torn trees and lines of blind men after the gas attacks.'

'Well, there're lines of youths now. They carry chains and bricks, and poor old Gladys is scared out of her wits. Apparently they started persecuting the two of them soon after Eddie left the police. Shoving parcels of . . . well, never mind what . . . but shoving them through the letter box. Gladys is too afraid to go out much now. She sort of looked to Macrae to help. Arrest the yobbos, that sort of thing.'

'Why don't you?'

'It's not on our manor, and anyway you've got to catch them at it. Can't arrest someone unless he's committed a crime – or at least you're pretty sure he has.'

'What about prevention being better than cure?'

'What about it?'

'Well, why wait until whatever happens happens? I mean if you know someone's going to be harmed or killed or whatever, wouldn't it be a good idea to stop it before you've got an injured person or a corpse?'

'You just can't go up to people and—'

'Come on, Leo. The police can do anything they like. You've told me so often enough.'

'Only by bending the rules. You wouldn't approve, and for that matter I wouldn't either.'

'You sound like the Archbishop of Canterbury. Sorry . . . I mean the Chief Rabbi.'

'Very amusing. Anyway Macrae did catch up with one youth and gave him a warning. Told him to lay off.'

'That doesn't sound like Macrae.'

'Well, there was a bit more to it than that.'

'Threats and menaces?'

21

'Sort of.'

'Will it do any good?'

'Shouldn't think so. Anyway, the whole thing's mainly Macrae's fault.'

'You know, Leo, sometimes you get a bit irrational about Macrae. He's been very good to you.'

'This hasn't anything to do with that. No . . . he didn't *mean* it. That's his trouble. He just doesn't *think* sometimes about other people.'

She thought of Leo's father and said, 'It's called being selfish. Go on.'

'Well, it's a kind of chain reaction. People of Macrae's rank always used to have drivers. Then there was the big reorganization of the Met to cut costs. No drivers any more. If you were going out on a job you went by Underground or bus or drove yourself.'

'Macrae? On a bus?' Her voice filled with awe.

'We travelled on the Underground together once. It was like *Star Trek*. New worlds. I don't think Macrae had been on a tube train for years. Kept on scowling at people. There was this young guy who was eating a doner kebab next to him. The smell wasn't too good. So Macrae tells him to put it away and the guy says mind your own business and Macrae tells him who he is and grabs him and marches him off the train at the next station and makes him eat the kebab right down at the end of the platform and then makes him find a litter basket and put everything in it – and only then lets him go.'

'I'm with Macrae. I hate people eating in trains and buses. Anyway what's that got to do with Eddie Twyford's funeral? You really must learn to think clearly, Leo.'

'I'm getting there. Well, Eddie was Macrae's driver in the old days. So to keep him Macrae gets him transferred around the department where he can drop everything when Macrae needs him. It's strictly against the rules but Macrae's such a good thief taker that no one complains.'

'Let me guess. Until Scales arrives.'

'Deputy Commander Kenneth Scales. The new broom. Right. He warns Macrae, not once but three or four times. Macrae ignores him. Finally Scales buries Eddie so deeply in the filing-room in Scotland Yard that there's no way Macrae can use him.

And Eddie hates it. It bores the pants off him.'

'So he resigns?'

'Retires. Goes home to live with Gladys on the Green Leas Estate and starts a long-running war with the local lads. The pressure and stress of it bring on a heart attack. And that's it.'

'That's what?'

'Well, the chain reaction.'

'So because Macrae doesn't like to travel next to people who eat doner kebabs, Eddie Twyford dies? Is that the scenario?'

'Something like that.'

'You'd better get into a different line of work—'

'Ssssh.'

'What?'

'I thought I heard something.'

'Goodnight, Leo.'

The following morning Leo was in the bathroom and Zoe was getting Manfred his breakfast of boiled eggs. Three and three-quarter minutes. Not three and a half. Not four. Three and three-quarters.

'Well?' Zoe said, standing over him as he broke the shells.

'Very nice.'

He said it grudgingly, as though he'd been rather hoping she would get it wrong.

He sipped his coffee suspiciously. He couldn't complain about that either. He looked at her over the cup. 'You don't have to lock your door here,' he said. 'It's not Pimlico.'

She was taken aback but, like a volley at the net, she replied, 'Didn't you know? Leo's afraid of ghosts.'

Manfred frowned and dipped his toast in his egg. He didn't really know how to handle Zoe. Her mother was said to be mad.

Like mother like daughter? He couldn't say, only that Zoe had always made him uneasy.

While Manfred Silver was testing his boiled eggs in West Hampstead, Detective Superintendent George Macrae was searching for a slim cigar in his small terraced house in Battersea. He found a packet, but it was empty. 'Bugger it!'

'What is it, George?' Frenchy called from the kitchen.

'Nothing.'

'You want more coffee?'

'No, thanks.'

He went into the sitting-room. A forensic team woud have had no difficulty in deciding what had taken place there the night before. The curtains were still drawn, there was an empty whisky bottle on the floor and a half-full bottle of Bacardi on the mantel-piece. A brassière lay on the carpet and a pair of woman's briefs hung from the branches of a yellowing umbrella plant.

Macrae opened the curtains and blinked in the harsh winter light, then began to search through the ashtrays. He found a cigar that had been half-smoked, straightened it, lit it, smoked it, and began to cough.

Frenchy came to the door. She was in her early twenties and was dressed in one of Macrae's shirts. It was open all the way down and showed a pair of large but firm breasts, a soft and creamy abdomen, and thighs and buttocks which might have been sculpted to suit Macrae's powerful hands. She was a simple crea-ture who spent a fair proportion of her time with him. It had started because her pimp owed him a favour but she had grown fond of him in a motherly sort of way.

'You want some breakfast, George?'

'No thanks.'

'You should eat something.'

'No thanks.'

'You want me to go out and buy a steak?'

'Jesus! At this time of day? What's this?'

It was a black leather bag with a shoulder strap, the size of a large flight bag. In their cavortings the night before it had fallen behind the sofa and some of its contents had spilled out.

'My work bag,' Frenchy said. She began to put the contents back. He saw soaps and shampoos, a tube of lubricant, face cloth, towel, two pairs of black lace panties, a black teddy, tampons, condoms, a diaphragm, lipstick and blusher, a couple of wigs, one red, one blonde, a telescopic whip, a pair of handcuffs, a vibrator, and a portaprinter for credit cards.

'I didn't know you took credit cards. I thought—'

'What, George?'

'I dunno. Thought it was a cash business I suppose.'

'Modelling fees. It's kosher. You're just old-fashioned.' She finished repacking and looked at her watch. 'I've got a couple of hours. You want to go back to bed?'

But George was not the man he once was.

She picked up the morning paper. 'I'm going to have a little peruse. I'll be upstairs if you feel like it.'

'Listen, I—'

The telephone rang.

'Is that Mr Macrae?'

'Who's that?'

'This is Mr Stoker.'

Macrae was puzzled for a moment. 'Mr . . . ?' Then he laughed harshly. 'Stoker? Is that you? Who gave you permission to call yourself "Mister", you horrible bastard?'

'There's no call for that, Mr Macrae.'

Stoker's voice was well controlled and Macrae should have guessed right then that something was up.

'Don't give me that crap, what d'you want?'

'Molly . . . Mrs Gorman would like to see you. She says can you come up to the house?'

'What's all this in aid of, Stoker?'

'Mrs Gorman will tell you.'

Macrae put the phone down. What did Stoker want and why hadn't Molly phoned him herself?

He relit the stale cigar and sat staring out at the winter street.

You thought things were over. That they were all right.

But they never were.

4

Click.

The light came on. She was glad, she had no wish to see the empty flat in the dusk of a winter's afternoon.

The sitting-room.

The sheet of paper from the estate agent called it a drawing-room, eighteen feet by fourteen, wood-block floors, fireplace, etc . . . etc . . .

She stood in the centre of the bare room lit by the single hanging bulb. A telephone sat on the floor. Old newspapers were piled against the wall.

She wasn't interested in wood-block floors or fireplaces. She wasn't interested in size or what the windows overlooked. She was interested in its aura, its smell. She was interested in what the walls told her, what the air told her.

Could you smell death? Terror? Despair?

The previous owner had died, the estate agent had said. They had instructions to let. Arrived in the post that very morning. Wasn't that a coincidence?

Wasn't what a coincidence?

That she should come in today, looking for a garden flat. This could be just the place.

He said he'd go with her.

But she said no. She'd go alone.

She saw his eyes change. She couldn't read them. He opened his mouth but the telephone rang. She took the keys and left.

And here she was in the drawing-room with the original ceiling-mouldings . . . etc . . . etc . . .

Houses were said to absorb the feelings of those who lived in them. It's such a happy house, people said.

26

Could the reverse be true?

Could she smell the fear? Had it been absorbed by the wallpaper and the plaster, and was it being slowly released?

She moved on through the rooms like a hand-held camera.

Click.

The bedroom. No wood-block floor here. Just the boards and a rectangle of dust on the floor where the bed had been.

Now she smelled something different: a mixture of stale perfume, talcum powder, and dust. Was that the smell of death? Was this where she had planned her death?

Or was it in the bathroom?

Click.

Slight smell of drains and damp. Slight smell of wet hair.

She wanted to know about the person in whose bedroom she would sleep, in whose bath she would bathe.

She wanted to know everything.

The taps were dripping, limescale had built up in the bath and basin. She'd have to do something about that. Couldn't live with dripping taps.

Click.

The kitchen.

Fridge . . . stove . . . Fixtures and fittings . . . What had she cooked on the stove? What had she kept in the fridge?

She opened it. All it contained was a bottle of water.

A glass door leads on to the patio and the garden, said the piece of paper.

No one had terraces any longer. Only patios.

She looked out at the garden, but in the fading light could see little: some spindly rose bushes, a shrub or two, pots of dead flowers. There was a plastic table and four plastic chairs.

Had she sat out here on summer evenings? Had there been the clink of ice in glasses? Talk? Suppers?

When she turned he was standing in the doorway behind her. She was afraid but did not show it.

He didn't want her to be alone in an empty flat, he said. Things happened to women in empty flats.

Linda Macrae let herself into her flat and locked the door behind her. Each evening when she came home from work this moment, when she switched on the lights, was one of intense pleasure. George had called her a nest-builder, and he was right. And even though her daughter Susan had flown the nest to live and travel with her boyfriend, and even though George had abandoned it many years before, it was still her nest.

This was a relatively new nest. Once Susan had gone she needed less space and could come nearer the heart of London. It had taken her a long time to find the flat in the converted house in Clapham, and, having found it, she knew she had to have it. It was *right* for her. But it would strain her finances. She thought it out for a whole ten minutes and what finally convinced her was the knowledge that she would be living alone and a woman living alone needed a safe refuge. She also needed a place – as George had once put it – that she could fiddle with.

She loved to fiddle, to move things around, to change one pot plant for another, to rearrange the sitting-room chairs, to put the stereo in the other corner. Often a whole weekend might pass in this way.

She had named this time of day 'the happy hour'. She would kick off her shoes, switch on the CD player – Chris de Burgh perhaps, or Eric Clapton, or maybe even one of the real oldies, Ella Fitzgerald or the Hot Club of France. Then she would pour herself a glass of wine and look through the TV listings for a movie or a soap.

But recently the happy hour had given way to the 'self-improvement hour'. Instead of Chris de Burgh, Fischer-Dieskau, instead of the Beatles, the London Symphony Orchestra. Tonight was opera night and she poured herself a glass of wine, put on *Turandot*, and opened the libretto.

But after a few moments her mind began to wander. The problems of Calaf and the three riddles seemed somehow remote this evening. An old familiar and unwelcome feeling began to steal over her. In the past she had fought it long and hard and thought she had banished it for ever. But here it was, lying in wait for her. It was called loneliness.

She began to pace restlessly round the flat. She moved a *Ficus* from one position to another. She was irritated with herself, for she knew the reasons for this return to the past. They were embodied in one personality called David Leitman who had come to live above her. He was an attractive man and it was a situation fraught with possibilities, pleasant or otherwise.

She had played things carefully. A few hellos and good mornings as they passed on the steps, but that was all. She had tied all the loose ends of her life together and didn't want them untied. She wasn't – and never had been – one for casual affairs: *ergo*, keep everything on a formal basis.

That, of course, had broken down. Leitman, recently divorced, was in need of company, as she had been when Macrae walked out on her. So it had begun with greetings, a friendly face, then a cup of coffee, a helping hand with a kitchen gadget. Coffee had become dinner; two Sunday lunches in a row had become an instant tradition.

'Look,' he had said to her. 'People of our age and situation don't simply hold hands. We have needs. We need each other. OK, we use each other. But that's what happens in life, people use people.'

And he was right, only . . . Well, she didn't want her life turned upside-down. That had happened once and she didn't want it to happen again. She'd tried the sexual therapy that men assured divorced women was so good for them and found one-night stands squalid. Once, waking up in a hotel in Surrey on a wet Sunday morning, she could not remember the name of the man who snored at her side.

It had never happened again.

And so she had been pussyfooting round Leitman like some nervous virgin. It was going to happen. It had to happen. But not just at this moment.

Carve it above her door: *Abandon Lust All Ye Who Enter Here*.

God, she thought, what a mixed-up cow.

She stopped moving plants about and looked at herself in a long wall-mirror. She was of medium height with brown hair and brown eyes. Her face had once been soft and pretty and was still attractive, but not soft any more. Her breasts were good, firm and high. Macrae, she remembered, had always been complimentary about her breasts, and he had a fixation about breasts.

She turned slightly. Bottom . . . well, never mind her bottom. Her legs had always been good and still were. Not bad for fortysomething. And it was nice to think she could interest a man like Leitman,

29

a writer whose life led him into areas and into contact with people she could only guess at. She had never known a writer before.

David loved books and music and it was only when she talked to him she realized her own ignorance. After Macrae had vanished from the nest with his new mistress, part of her vacuum had been filled by self-improving books. She had continued reading until they were no longer chores but much-loved companions. Now it was all happening again with music.

'You fancy him,' she said to herself. 'You want him. You're doing all this just because of him.'

And just because of him she was lonely. The previous day he had left for Scotland to research a book. There was an unspoken agreement that both would consider their position during this absence.

All right, I've considered, she thought. If he came through the door now I'd lead him straight into the bedroom. Then she said aloud, 'Why don't I have a lovely chicken sandwich, instead?' As the sound of her voice died, she thought she heard knocking. Not at her door. But somewhere in the depths of the house.

She stood quite still, listening intently. She was alone. David was somewhere in the Highlands and the garden flat had been empty for weeks.

She opened her front door on the chain. The tapping was louder and was coming from beneath her in the garden flat. Her staircase, which she shared with David, was dark. Should she switch on the light and go and investigate? But what if there was someone there? An intruder? A burglar?

But what burglar in his right mind would break into an empty flat and start to make a noise?

Squatters? Her heart sank. She had lived near squatters once before and hoped never to do so again.

She took off the chain, put on the hall light, and went down to the street door. On each side of the door were little coloured windows. She could see out into the basement area. Light was reflected there.

She listened intently. If there was more than one person she would have expected to hear voices. But all was silent. Even the tapping had stopped.

The lights suddenly went out, the area became dark. She heard the front door of the garden flat open and close then sharp footsteps on the outside stairs. A woman dressed in a long dark coat came up the steps and went down the path to the street. She opened the gate and disappeared. A moment later Linda heard a car engine start.

She went back to her flat and was closing the door when the phone rang. The sudden noise froze her blood.

'Hi,' the voice said. 'It's me, David.'

She was confused for a moment and then suddenly embarrassed as though he might read her mind and discover her recent thoughts.

'Where are you?' she said.

'Just south of Inverness. I'm staying at a fishing hotel. It might be OK in summer but I'm the only guest and it's like living inside a mausoleum.'

She wanted to react, to be amused, but she was still anxious.

'I've just had my dinner,' he said. 'Some kind of thin soup with barley in it. Cod in parsley sauce. Jam roly-poly. In total silence. Each mouthful watched by the waitress. The moment I put down my cutlery she tried to take the plate away. Wanting to get off home, I suppose.'

'It sounds gruesome.'

'It is. I'm phoning from the bar. Not another soul. I miss you.'

'That's nice.'

'You're supposed to say I miss you too.'

'Well, I do. The house is so . . . '

'Empty? I tried to talk you into coming with me.'

'I know.' Pause. 'David—'

'What?'

'Someone's been in the garden flat.' She told him what she had heard and seen.

'Well, she wouldn't be a burglar. They don't break into empty flats.'

'That's what I thought.'

'See if the sign's gone.'

She went to the window. 'David, it has! I never even noticed.'

'That's it, then. New tenant.'

'I hope she's luckier than the last one.'

'I hope so too.'

31

5

Cannon Row police station stands on the north bank of the Thames in the centre of London. It is part Victorian Gothic, part functional modern. The old part is a warren of corridors, the new part is filled with high-tech equipment. It has a small car park which is guarded by high walls and steel security gates; its glass windows are bomb-proof.

If you want to know the time don't try to ask a policeman in Cannon Row; stand on the nearby Embankment lawns and look up at Big Ben. It is only a stone's throw away.

London is divided into eight police Areas. Cannon Row is the brains, the liver and the lights, the viscera, of Area One.

Macrae parked his elderly Rover and went in to see his immediate chief, Detective Chief Superintendent Leslie Wilson. He found him cleaning his shoes. Macrae hardly registered. Wilson had been regularly cleaning his shoes since they had joined the Force together more years ago now than Macrae cared to think about.

It had begun when they were both beat coppers and both had to keep their boots clean. But once he had become a detective, Macrae had lapsed into suede shoes. Wilson found the cleaning action therapeutic and had continued. He always wore black half-brogues, always wore a dark grey suit. No one had ever seen him in brown shoes or without a tie. He was a neat man.

'Morning, George.'

Macrae nodded and went to the window. Wilson's office had a view of the Thames but on this misty morning only vague outlines could be discerned.

'Bloody fog,' Macrae said. 'These days it only takes one accident south of the river and every bridge is solid.'

'Want some coffee?'

'Anything stronger?'

'Christ, no! And you shouldn't even be thinking about it at this time of the morning.'

'You don't get cirrhosis *thinking* about it.'

Wilson wondered if he was starting this early. He knew Macrae had always liked a drop – well, who didn't? Once they'd all had a bottle in their bottom drawers. But then the brass at Scotland Yard had come down on drinking in the office – and out of it for that matter – and Deputy Commander Kenneth Scales had arrived at Cannon Row to carry out this bizarre edict. Scales was the perfect man for the job; tomato juice with Worcestershire sauce was his tipple.

Wilson, like many other senior officers, had cleared the Famous Grouse from his desk and had placed a moratorium on long pub lunches until the good times returned.

But not Macrae. You only had to tell him something, Wilson thought, for him to do the exact opposite. Well, he'd warned him often enough that his promotion depended on keeping a clean sheet. But telling him was one thing, getting him to act on it quite another. He knew – and he knew George knew he knew – that it should have been Macrae sitting behind Scales's desk. But what the hell, life was like that. There were always people who were their own worst enemies no matter what the talent.

'You weren't at Eddie's funeral.' Macrae's tone was accusatory.

'I hardly knew him. Anyway, I sent flowers to what's her name? The wife.'

'The widow. Gladys.'

'How was it?'

'They dig a hole. Put you in a coffin. Bury you.'

Wilson put away his shoeshine kit. His nervous eyes, which had earned him the nickname 'Shifty', flickered around the room. 'OK, George . . . I've got work to—'

'Never mind that, Les. I'm telling you it was bloody sad. Silver, me, Gladys – and the other three were paid to be there. I mean that's bloody terrible. A whole life gone down the drain. And you know why?'

Yes, he knew why, it was like the bloody Nuns' Chorus. Kept coming back.

'Scales!'

Wilson hurriedly closed his door. These confrontations with Macrae always upset him, especially in the morning. Buggered his whole day. If it wasn't that Macrae was so good at his job – which, he had to admit, rubbed off on him as well – he'd have sent him to some remote Siberia of the Force in the same way that Scales had exiled Eddie Twyford. But Macrae was different. He was known as a thief taker. And yet . . . Even that was going to rebound on him one day.

If for nothing else, there were his methods. They were old style. To hell with the new rules of evidence, to hell with the recent court rulings on uncorroborated confessions, to hell with everything about modern policing . . . If someone was guilty Macrae *knew* it, could *smell* it, and if he needed to put the frighteners on a suspect to get an admission, he did.

The problem for everyone else was that Macrae was usually right. He had the best informants in town, the best network of information. And the other thing, the A-plus factor, was that he had never had his hand in the till. There had never been a whisper of him taking a backhander.

But, and Wilson thought it was a big but, who wanted coppers like Macrae these days? The theory went that it was better for fifty villains to go free than for one innocent man to be imprisoned. So you did things by the book. And if you didn't pick up the villains, what did it matter? You'd done it by the book. Sooner or later just doing things by the book would bring society to a standstill – that was Macrae's attitude, and he had expressed it often enough in tones loud and clear – and in Scales' hearing.

There was open warfare now between Scales and Macrae. It had started with Eddie Twyford but if that hadn't been the spark it would have been something else. The chemistry between them was flawed. At first Wilson thought Scales might put up with Macrae because the big man was the best detective in Area One and Scales basked in the radiance that drew. But then there had been the incident involving Scales' mother and that had finally caused an irreparable breach.

It had happened a couple of months before. Scales was to get the Queen's Police Medal – an award made to about twenty senior officers a year – and Macrae had been loudly contemptuous.

'They get it for turning up for work,' he had said to Wilson.

'You don't have to *do* anything, Les. Just turn up and keep your nose clean. He's an almost-and-nearly man. Can't make a decision by himself so he forms a committee. *And* he's a bloody apron-lifter.'

This was Macrae's phrase for Freemasons, who held many of the plum positions in the Force. He pretended not to know that Wilson was himself a Mason. Indeed Wilson had once, in a moment of aberration, considered proposing Macrae, but had prudently reconsidered. Now the thought of Macrae being blind-folded and pricked and generally being 'on the square' gave him nervous indigestion.

Scales' award party had been held in the canteen at Cannon Row. Thirty or forty officers with their wives or girlfriends had attended, and a congratulatory speech had been made by an assistant commissioner. Scales had been toasted in sparkling wine by everyone except his mother, who had toasted him in Perrier water.

It had been an uneasy affair. Usually an award party, like a retirement party, was an excuse for a bash where everyone got drunk and started groping each others' wives or girlfriends, or the women police officers. But with Scales clutching his tomato juice, and his mother her Perrier, it was like having two spectres at the feast.

Scales, with his bony face and hair combed across his balding skull, had always reminded Macrae of a death's head. Mother resembled son. She was grey and gnarled with thin bloodless lips and reminded Macrae of parishioners of the Free Presbyterian Church of his Scottish childhood who frowned on anything to do with pleasure.

It was into this staid scene that Macrae and Frenchy burst. They were late, and it was obvious that both had been drinking.

'What's this?' Macrae had said, sniffing the cheap sparkling wine which Scales had produced. 'It smells like camel's—'

'Evening, George.' Wilson hurriedly inserted himself between Macrae and Scales.

'Where's the Scotch?'

'Why don't you have a nice glass of sparkling Liebfraumilch instead?'

'Fuck that. Here Les, you mind Frenchy for me. And no touch-ing, laddie.'

He went out of the room and Wilson could see Scales' head turn to watch him.

'George likes his whisky,' Frenchy said.

'What about you?'

'I don't mind. I'm partial to most things.'

He gave her a glass of wine, which she sipped modestly, her little finger raised.

Wilson's shifty eyes travelled up and down her body. Jesus Christ, how did George do it? Here Wilson was, under the eye of Beryl, his wife of nearly twenty years, who wore curlers and cotton gloves to bed, and here was Macrae, shagging this voluptuous piece who seemed to be on the point of bursting out of her skimpy clothing.

Macrae came back with a flask, poured himself half a glass of neat whisky, said, 'Slainté,' took it in one swallow, and said, 'That's a wee bit better.'

Wilson lost Macrae and Frenchy for half an hour. When he saw them again he went cold.

Scales had disappeared – as he later discovered, to fetch his mother's coat and scarf – and Macrae, with the better part of a flask of whisky inside him, on top of what he had drunk earlier, was being sociable to Mrs Scales.

As Wilson tried to reach them, he heard Macrae say, 'There's nothing like a good hot vindaloo . . . '

'And he usually asks for chilli sauce to go with it,' Frenchy put in.

'I like to sweat below the eyes when I eat curry,' Macrae said.

'I must be getting home,' Mrs Scales said, looking round desperately for her son.

'I'm perspiring right now,' Frenchy said.

'They have the heating up too high,' Macrae said. 'Take your jacket off, love.'

'Kenneth's gone off to fetch my things,' Mrs Scales said for the second or third time.

'And find them he will, ma'am,' Macrae said with a little bow. 'He is a detective.'

He held Frenchy's glass as she removed her coat. All she was wearing underneath was a lacy top of some fine flesh-coloured material. It was so transparent that at first glance Wilson thought

36

she was naked. Her two large breasts became the focus of his attention as they did to several other police officers standing near by.

They were, indeed, superb objects, Wilson thought. Although larger than average they stood out proud and firm without aid of bra, the jutting nipples penetrating the lacy fabric like two inquisitive pink noses.

In the immediate neighbourhood a silence fell. It was deeply admiring.

Macrae, like some sculptor who has just unveiled his masterpiece, turned to Mrs Scales, and, indicating Frenchy's lovely bust, said, 'Magnificent, aren't they? I've always maintained that there's nothing as sad as a drooping tit.'

Mrs Scales' lips became a thin white line. Her son pushed his way through the mob with her coat and she thrust her hands into the sleeves.

'Good night to you, dear lady,' Macrae said with his little bow. But Mrs Scales did not reply.

Now, recalling the incident with a shudder, Wilson looked at the big man. His face was beginning to sag a little, his eyes were bloodshot, and there was a kind of seediness about him that men without a live-in woman often developed.

In this conflict between the two men Wilson found himself caught in the middle. He didn't like Scales, but that was beside the point. Scales had been sent to Cannon Row to do a job – to cut expenditure mainly – but also, as he was fond of repeating, to drag the Met into the twenty-first century.

The problem was that Macrae was distinctly twentieth, someone who had been frozen about 1978 when the Met did its own thing and to hell with public opinion.

The dear dead days of yore, as Macrae had named them. Well, as far as Scales was concerned they were dead and buried too.

A couple of years ago Wilson would have backed Macrae against Scales. Now he wasn't so sure. The tide seemed to be running against the big man.

'What d'you know about a villain called Stoker?' Macrae asked.

'That cowboy from the Angel?'

'The same.'

Wilson was known as the memory man. Just as there were

37

football fans who could tell you how many left-handed Methodists had played for Manchester United in 1968, so Les Wilson could tell you the ages and middle names of everyone connected with the Great Train Robbery. Macrae could just about see a light switch on behind Wilson's eyes.

'He put one of our lads in hospital a couple of years back. Hit him with a tyre lever.'

'And before that?'

'The usual. Joy riding, then nicking cars to order. Robbery. Burglary. Why?'

'I just wondered.'

Wilson scowled at him. Macrae never 'just wondered' about anything. 'You going to tell me?'

'Nothing to tell. He's living with Artie Gorman's widow, Molly.'

'I met her once. Good-looking woman. She must be years older than him. Never knew what she saw in that little bookie.'

'Artie? He was all right.'

'Come on, he was as bent as a safety-pin.'

'What about Stoker? Any recent form?'

'Not that I know of. Anyway, if you did a CRO search you'd know yourself. By the way, didn't Scales want you to go on a computer course? You should, you know. Make your record look good.'

'Do me a favour, Les.' He moved to the door.

Wilson said, 'If you had your way we'd go back to file cards and wind-up clocks. Time marches on, George.'

'So they tell me.'

She liked the flat, she said, but there were problems.

Problems? He thought she'd agreed, that's why he'd removed the To Let sign.

No, she hadn't agreed. He'd been mistaken there.

He was in his mid-thirties, she thought, of medium height. She had noticed he wore built-up heels, otherwise he would have been no taller than herself. He was light-skinned and wore a heavy moustache and was quite sharply dressed in a soft grey suit and mauve shirt. His tie was flowered.

He was making a statement about himself. His clothes said he was youngish and trendy. The moustache lent severity to a face that might otherwise have been weak. It said: I may be an estate agent who has to eat shit in these hard times, but don't let that fool you.

What were these problems, then?

Well, there was the damp in the bathroom, the limescale, the dripping taps, there was worn and torn lino in the kitchen.

He jotted all this down. Part of him, she thought, was unctuous, part aggressive.

He was sure everything could be worked out.

Oh, but that wasn't all.

They went through the flat, she picking on detail, he making notes.

She asked him about the previous tenant.

She had been young, he said. It was a tragedy.

What had she died of?

He didn't know, only that it had been sudden.

Here?

No, no. In hospital. Certainly not here.

They walked from room to room.

The price, she said, was unrealistic in these hard times.

He didn't like that. She knew it would reduce his commission to go lower.

The price was the price, he said. He had no instructions to bargain.

In that case she'd pass on this one. There were others in the area.

Well, hang on, he didn't say he wouldn't try. He'd see what he could do. Speak to the owner.

He knew the owner?

Well, not the owner exactly, but the owner's representatives. He would phone them. Why not drop round to the office later, see if there was any news.

When she did go back it was done; not easily, he said, but done. A meeting of minds in these hard times.

Since Eddie died Gladys had developed a pattern. First of all she checked the lock on her front door, then her back door. Thank God Eddie had had deadlocks fitted. She had wondered at the time whether they should have asked permission from Mr Geach, the housing manager. It stated in the contract that no alterations, structural or otherwise, could be made in the flats without permission. It was well known that Mr Geach hardly ever gave permission.

'What if he doesn't let us?' Eddie had said. 'To hell with him.'

Eddie had always been like that, she thought. Strong. Decisive. It was the way he drove a car. Knew every street, every short cut. You couldn't tell Eddie anything about driving in London. Even Mr Macrae said that, and he never, or hardly ever, praised anyone. That's what Eddie had told her, and she believed it.

And now he was gone! Her eyes filled with tears. They seemed to do that constantly nowadays. She couldn't stop herself.

'Come on, Gladys,' she said to herself through bulldog. 'Get a move on.'

As she checked the locks she was glad Eddie had never asked permission. What if Mr Geach *had* said no?

'We'd have been unprotected. Both of us.'

She checked the lock on the back door and then began to drag the kitchen table across the floor. She wedged it against the door and put the two kitchen chairs on top of it. Then the bread tin. Then several pots and pans.

If they tried to come in that way they'd first of all have to push the table out of the way. The chairs would fall, so would everything else. The noise would be enough to wake the dead and it would give her time to call the police.

When she was satisfied with the kitchen she began to work on her bedroom. She brought in the telephone on its long cord. Filled the kettle. Saw that her sandwiches were on the bedside table, that the TV and radio were plugged in. That bulldog was on the windowsill.

She closed the bedroom door, bolted it, and dragged the foot of the bed against it. Then she opened the wardrobe, brought out her chamber pot, and put it under the bed.

By the time she had done all this she was exhausted. But the place, as far as she could make it, was secure. It was not quite four o'clock in the afternoon and Gladys was getting ready for bed.

6

This was the time Macrae missed Eddie Twyford. Stuck in a traffic jam in Baker Street. If Eddie had been driving they would (a) not have got into the traffic jam at all, he would have known some short cut that would have taken them clear of it, or (b) if they *had* got stuck they would have had an argument about why and so passed the time. Or Macrae would have lit up a slim panatella and opened the *Daily Telegraph* and ignored the whole business.

As it was he couldn't do any of these, not even the cigar, for the packet was in his overcoat and that was on the back seat with all the other bits and pieces – old newspapers, old cardigans, old this and that – which had been flung on to the back seat over the years and forgotten.

The traffic moved and Macrae moved with it. His thoughts remained on Eddie and Gladys. He was sorry for her, but, as he had told Silver, what the hell was he supposed to do about it? You made your decisions in life and you had to accept them.

He remembered how happy Eddie had been to get one of the low-rental flats on the Green Leas Estate. At that time Macrae's second wife Mandy had recently left him and had been granted maintenance for herself and the two kids and he had been envious of Eddie and his cheap accommodation, his one and only wife, his childless life. It had been in such contrast to his own existence.

And now look what had happened.

You could never tell who was going to be the lucky punter. Not that Macrae considered himself lucky; not with his financial problems.

What the bloody hell did Stoker want?

The last time he had gone to Artie Gorman's house, the little

41

bookie had been dying. Well, now he was dead. So why was Stoker still there? That's if he *was* still there. And why had he become Molly's mouthpiece?

The house was in Gospel Oak. It was double fronted and stood in its own garden. Had to be worth a fortune, Macrae thought, even in a recession.

Molly came to the door. 'Hello, George. Come in.'

He had always fancied Molly. She was in her forties. Blonde, brassy, but genuine. Now he hardly recognized her. She was dressed in a miniskirt and long boots, her hair was dark, had a henna sheen and was done in a mass of crimped curls. Her skin, with the unmistakable bloom of a sunlamp on it, looked leathery in the hard winter light.

She put up her cheek to be kissed and he saw the expression in her eyes. She knew what he must be thinking: mutton dressed as lamb.

'What's it all about, Molly?'

'Gary wants to see you.'

'Gary? Oh, Stoker. He said *you* wanted to see me.'

'Well . . . he's the one, really. He's looking after my . . . our business interests.' She looked away, unable to meet his eyes. 'He's out in Artie's old office in the garden.'

'Hang on a sec. Let me get something straight. Is Stoker handling your business affairs?'

'Yes, George.'

'Listen, I've got to have a word.'

'In here then.'

She took him into her drawing-room. It was all flock wallpaper and original Tretchikoffs and shrieked of money badly spent. She indicated a sofa covered in grass-green velvet, but he shook his head.

'How long have we known each other, Molly?'

'What's this, all our yesterdays?'

'It's got to be fifteen years. I mean you married Artie—'

'Nearly twenty years ago and he was twenty years older than me. What's it all in aid of?'

'I'm bothered about you. I'm seeing something I don't like.'

'It's got nothing to do with you, George.'

'I'm a policeman. I think like a policeman. Lads like Stoker are my meat and drink.'

'Only when they've done something.'

'Oh, he's done lots, Molly. Let me tell you—'

She put her hands to her ears. 'Stop it!'

'Molly!'

'Stop it! Stop it! I don't want to hear.'

He pulled her hands away and held them for a moment in one of his. 'You're going to listen. At least I owe Artie that. I suppose you're living with Stoker.'

When she didn't reply, he said, 'That's your business, but I think you should know the sort of man he is. A few years ago he broke the arm of one of our lads. Uniformed PC in Hackney. This young laddie had only been on the force a short while and he comes across Stoker loading stuff into a car about three o'clock in the morning. So he asks him what it's all about and Stoker takes a tyre lever to him. Then bends his arm back so it breaks at the—'

'I don't want to hear! Anyway I don't believe it.'

She sat down suddenly.

'You don't believe it because you don't want to believe it. But it's true.'

He paused, then said, 'Listen, Molly, you don't need people like Stoker around.'

'What do you know about my needs? Nothing! Not a bloody thing!'

'Maybe I shouldn't have said that. But I always thought how lucky you and Artie—'

'Don't go on about it.'

'But it's true. You were lucky. I envied you your marriage.'

She smiled bitterly. 'Did you?'

'I know Artie was a wee bit bent. But not like Stoker.'

'Gary's made me happy, George.'

'Happy? How?'

'Artie was impotent.'

'Oh.'

'You asked. I told you.'

'And that's all it is? Sex?'

43

'All? You must be getting old, George.'

'Listen, Artie brought Stoker in as a minder. To mind you while he went about the business of dying. He told me so himself. Told me he didn't want you vulnerable to any bloody cowboy who might grab you and hold you to ransom. Stoker's as thick as two planks.'

'You can stop it now, George.'

'Looking after your business affairs! Christ!' He paused, shaking his head in disbelief, then said, 'Artie must have left you well provided for. Stoker will have the lot. You think he's living with you because he loves you? Forget it. People like Stoker don't—'

She rose suddenly. 'That's enough!' Her face was stiff with anger. 'Gary's waiting for you.'

Artie's office was at the end of the back garden. It was more a Tyrolean chalet than a garden hut and all it lacked was a pair of chamois horns above the door. Stoker was sitting in Artie's chair behind Artie's desk. His feet were stretched out so he could show off his cowboy boots. The rest of him was denim and gold chains.

'Molly tells me it's you who wants a chat,' Macrae said. 'If I'd known that I wouldn't have bothered to come.'

Stoker looked younger than Macrae had remembered. There were several scars on his face and hands, not big ones, but enough to give a hint of violence.

'Sit down, Mr Macrae.'

Macrae didn't deign to register that he had heard. 'What do you want, Stoker?'

'Nice, innit?' Stoker said, embracing the garden-room. There were two VDUs to the left of the desk.

'I liked it when Mr Gorman had it,' Macrae said, emphasizing the word 'mister'. Two could play at this game.

'Reuters',' Stoker said, pointing to one of the VDUs. 'The other's the Extel.'

He pressed a remote-control button and one of the screens changed. 'Dow Jones whatsits.' He pressed again. 'American long bond in Far East trading.'

'What's the point of it all?'

'The point? The point is I can see what the money-markets are doing. That's the point.'

'But how does that help you?'

Stoker frowned. 'You gotta know what the money-markets are doing if you're a player.'

'But that presupposes you can read, Stoker. You can read, can you? I didn't know that. I always thought – when I thought about you at all, which wasn't very often – I always thought you were illiterate. Now you tell me you can read. I'm glad about that, laddie. In Scotland we have a great respect for education.'

Stoker said, 'Have your fun, Mr Macrae.'

'Get on with it, you miserable shit.'

'Right, Mr Macrae. Fine.'

He opened a drawer and took out a large brown ledger. His finger travelled down the columns. 'Yeah, here it is. George Macrae. Three thousand quid.'

Macrae had guessed it had something to do with the money and now his large head dropped slightly further forward. 'What's that got to do with you, Stoker?'

'We don't like bad debts. Stands to reason.'

'You're running the business, are you?'

'Didn't Mrs Gorman explain? You were with her long enough.'

'Her business manager. Is that it?'

'That's a way of puttin' it.'

'Come on, Stoker, you know bugger-all about business. Your idea of a takeover is to stick a gun in someone's ear and take his money.'

'The simple methods are the best methods, Mr Macrae.'

'Let me tell you something, you little turd—'

'Hold on, Mr Macrae. There's no call for that. I don't insult you. Please do me the same favour. And I know what you're gonna say. You're gonna tell me that the last time you came here Mr Gorman said he was wiping out the debt; that he didn't want you upset about it.'

'That's right, Stoker, that's what he said.'

'Money for your daughter, wasn't it? Didn't she want to go round the world or somethin'?'

'Leave her out of it!'

'Anything you say, Mr Macrae.'

'You've put Molly up to this! She'd never have thought of it in a million years.'

'She's far too kind-hearted for business matters. I've told her

45

that before.' He took an audio cassette from the drawer, turned to a line of cupboards behind him, opened one, and Macrae saw a cassette deck.

Stoker slipped in the tape and pressed the PLAY button. There was the noise of a door closing, then Artie's voice saying, *'Hello, George, come on in.'*

Macrae felt his back hair rise. It was not only hearing the dead man's voice. He knew exactly when and where this had been recorded. It was the last time he had seen Artie.

Stoker ran the tape forward. 'We can get over the chit-chat.' He looked at the counter and restarted the tape. 'Listen to this.'

Artie's voice said, *'Affairs, George. Getting them in order. That's what I want to talk to you about.'*

'Artie, I know what you're going to say and I—'

'George, you haven't a clue what I'm going to say. I wanted to see you to tell you that I don't want the three thousand—'

Stoker ran the tape on and Artie's voice said, *'I told you when I lent you the money: three thousand isn't heavy for me . . .'*

Stoker stopped the tape. 'Who'd have thought Mr Gorman would put it all on tape? But he did. In his last months he put everything on tape. Kind of insurance, see.'

Macrae was staring at the cassette deck.

Stoker said, 'We want the money, Mr Macrae.'

Macrae didn't miss the emphasis on the word 'we'.

He looked at the tape cassette in Stoker's hand. 'You want it?' Stoker said. 'You can have it. It's only a copy.'

'You can go and get fucked,' Macrae said.

'That's bluff. You know it. I know it.'

'I don't give a toss what you call it. I haven't got three thousand quid and even if I had there's no way—'

'Oh, it ain't three thousand. There's been interest, see. We're looking at six, George, and risin'.'

Macrae stood over him. He felt a surge of powerful anger go into his hands. He wanted to lean over and take Stoker by the throat and squeeze the life out of him.

'I know what you're thinkin', George.'

'Do you?'

'Course I do. I'd be thinkin' it meself.'

46

'As long as you know.'

'Yeah. And at any other time I'd be right worried. But I've got insurance now, George. I'm sure we can work things out. Even if you ain't got the money. Payment in kind, so to speak.'

Macrae laughed. It was not much of a laugh. 'You must be out of what passes for your mind, Stoker.'

He turned on his heel and walked out of the room and down the garden.

'Think about it, George,' Stoker called after him.

Stoker stood at the drawing-room windows watching Macrae climb into the Rover.

'Shithead!' he said.

Molly joined him.

'Look at him!'

Macrae was wrestling with the car, trying to get out of a tight space. Behind it was a gold Rolls-Royce. Suddenly Stoker gripped the curtains. 'If he touches the Roller it's another grand.'

But Macrae managed to get out without damaging any other vehicle and disappeared down the street in a haze of blue smoke.

'Calls himself a copper. Can't even drive properly.'

'He always had someone to drive for him.'

'The Jewboy?'

'No, not Silver, an older man. Drove him for years and years. Gary . . . '

'Yeah?'

'Gary, listen, I don't like doing this to George. He was a good friend to Artie. They went back a long way; to when George was on the beat and Artie was a bookie's runner.'

'You can't be "good friends" with coppers.'

'I know that. It's just—'

'You're not scared of Macrae, are you?'

'I respect him. And you'd better too. There's something about him. He's not like other coppers. He's unpredictable. And he's got brains even though he doesn't show them.'

'So've I.'

She turned away so he wouldn't see her expression.

He pinched the soft skin under her arm.

47

'You're hurting me!'

'Nah . . . I wouldn't hurt you.' He pinched again. 'Get us a drink.' She rubbed her arm, then opened a can of Foster's and poured herself a large vodka on the rocks. 'For Christ's sake take something with it. Orange juice. Tomato juice. Something.'

'I like it like this.'

'I don't like to fuck drunks. Never did fancy it.'

'You've got a nasty mouth, Gary.'

He showed her the tip of his pink tongue. 'You said you liked it.'

She turned away. 'You've changed. You weren't like this when Artie was alive.'

'It's you that's changed. Come here.'

Reluctantly she moved towards him. He caught her hand and pulled her down on to the sofa with him. Her miniskirt had ridden up and he slipped his hand between her thighs.

'Not here,' she said.

'Yeah. Here. Now.'

'They can see us through the windows.'

'Who?'

'People in the houses opposite.'

'Let them. Do 'em good.'

He unbuttoned her blouse and began to stroke her breasts. He kissed her. It was like switching on a power supply.

'You changed your mind?' he said.

'Yes.'

'You want to?'

'Yes.'

'Really want to?'

'Really want to.'

He pushed her away and got up. 'Keep it warm,' he said. 'I'm just going out to buy a packet of fags.'

She watched him go out of the house and along the street. He was walking slowly, as though he had all the time in the world. Slowly she buttoned her blouse and straightened her clothes. Then she lit a cigarette from his packet on the coffee table. Her hands were shaking. She sat smoking and looking at the wall. How had things got like this? she wondered.

*

48

Macrae was hardly conscious of where he was. He saw a parking space, pulled up and parked. He was in Camden Town and he wanted a drink. He went into the nearest pub, an anonymous place with fruit machines and canned music. He ordered a large Scotch, downed it, ordered another, and took it to a table. He lit a panatella and sipped the Scotch.

What happened next?

Well, in the movies the scenario might go something like this: you set Stoker up and killed him. Simple. Indeed, Stoker himself had said the simple methods were the best methods.

A bullet between the ears and who'd know or care?

Molly would know and care.

So shoot Molly too.

And then the bank manager who was holding the original tape – or was it a lawyer? – would know and care. So kill them.

Macrae had no particular moral inhibitions about the thought of lawyers or bank managers dying violent deaths, it was just that the number of those who might know and care would increase exponentially to the point where whole families, then whole professions, might have to be removed.

So . . . Stoker couldn't be killed, indeed couldn't even be frightened off, since he was the one who was doing the frightening.

The alternative was to pay the money. Six thousand quid. He didn't have it or any prospect of getting it.

He took out his pen and notebook and started to jot down the names of people who might lend him six thousand. At the end of ten minutes he had jotted down just three names. He stared at them. Slowly the knowledge crept over him that they were all villains of one sort of another.

There wasn't an honest man among them.

Was this what his life had become?

He bought another large Scotch and nursed it. This was the dangerous one. This would give him the taste, the need. If he wasn't careful, this was the one that would drop him into the old familiar abyss where the next drink wasn't measured out in a bar but poured out from his own bottle in his own house.

You can't afford a binge, he told himself. Not with people like Stoker about.

The third alternative, the one that sat just on the edge of his conscious mind, hardly bore thinking about. Payment in kind, Stoker had said. And Macrae knew exactly what that would mean. He'd be on the payroll. First the six thousand would be wiped off 'for favours received' – small things at first like getting information from the police computer or looking the other way when something untoward happened on his manor.

But then would come the hard cash. Monthly. In an envelope. Handed to him in a men's lavatory or a car park in Surrey.

He'd be a bent copper.

Stoker would bend him.

The fact was there wasn't anything he could do at the moment except wait and see.

7

'My name is Irene,' the woman said.

She was standing on the steps leading up to the front door of the house and had pressed Linda Macrae's bell. 'I'm sorry to disturb you, but I wanted to introduce myself and I heard you come in.'

'The garden flat!' Linda said. 'So you moved in today? I saw the lights. Won't you come in?'

'No, really, I—'

'Please, I was about to make some coffee.'

'That's kind of you,' Irene said. 'Only a minute.' She entered the flat. 'What a lovely room.'

It was a large room running from the front of the house to the rear and patterned with shadows made by spotlamps on greenery.

Irene followed her into the kitchen. Linda said, 'I was just about to come downstairs to see if there was anything you needed.'

She looked at her new neighbour while she poured boiling water into the filter. She was about her own age, with a sallow skin and eyes that were almost black. Her hair, which glinted and shone in the lights, was pulled back. She wore glasses and a shapeless fisherman's sweater, which covered her body down to her thighs. There was something . . . something not quite right about her, Linda thought, but couldn't tell what it was.

'Moving is so awful I don't know why we do it,' Irene said.

'Where have you moved from?'

They took the coffee into the sitting-room.

'I've lived in so many places.'

She leaned back in the chair and put the mug of coffee down on the table. Her gestures were smooth, elegant; her hands were beautiful, strong and finely kept, the nails immaculate, not too

51

long, not too short. They shone like her hair.

They seemed so out of keeping with the casual way she was dressed that Linda had to remind herself that she had only moved in that day.

Her face behind the glasses was sensual, her body supple, languid. She gave the impression of being a dancer but she was not lean enough. Then Linda suddenly thought of Egypt. She had been there on holiday once. Irene reminded her of a belly-dancer, sinuous and supple, fleshy without being fat, with a full body and full breasts.

They talked amiably for a while, discussing the usual formalities: which dairy delivered milk in this street, which newsagents the papers. Linda began to relax. If you had to have neighbours then Irene looked like a good prospect. David above and Irene below. Then abruptly she thought, oh-oh; three loose cannons in the same house.

'Sorry?' She had missed Irene's last question.

'I was asking about my predecessor. Did you know her?'

'Not really. By sight, of course, but I hardly saw her. Her name was Grace.'

'Nice name.'

'It didn't do her much good.'

'Oh?'

'Well, for one thing, she's dead.'

'Yes, the estate agent mentioned that.'

'Gerald?'

'Is that his name?'

'Gerald Masters. Of Marshall and Masters.'

'Did you get your flat through him?' Irene said.

Linda nodded. 'He has most of this area. He's into property as well. Buying and selling.'

Irene drained her coffee and made as though to rise. 'I must—'

'There's no hurry. This is my self-improvement hour. I don't mind missing it. More coffee?'

'Half, then.'

Linda poured it from the filter and added cream. Irene helped herself to sugar, then said, 'What did Grace die of?'

'We were never quite sure.'

'We?'

52

'David . . . Mr Leitman. He lives upstairs. He's away at the moment. All I know is an ambulance came for her one morning.'

'Strange, isn't it?'

'What?'

'Life in a big city. Or maybe I should say death. People live in capsules. No one cares what happens to them.'

'We cared.' It was sharply said, for Linda felt resentful at the implied lack of feeling. 'We tried several times to befriend her. She didn't want us. It was sad because she seemed so alone. But she must have had her reasons.'

She was remembering the last time. The noises had been louder than before. Not the noise of the music, that hadn't bothered her for she had only to turn hers up to drown it. No, it had been the noise of violence that had caused them to investigate. She and David had stood in the front hall listening to the noise in the basement.

'This is bloody terrible,' he had said. 'I'm going down.'

She had gone with him in case her help was needed. It took Grace some time to answer the bell. She was painfully thin with a large-eyed, pre-Raphaelite beauty, sad and tormented. Her face was marked, her lips were swollen, and she had been weeping.

'Yes?'

David said, 'We heard . . . well, noises. We wondered if you were all right.'

'I'm fine.'

Linda had sensed a man in the background but had not seen him.

'Are you sure?' Linda had said.

'Yes, I'm sure.' The subtext was: 'Why don't you mind your own business?'

Grace had closed the door and that had been that.

Now Linda repeated, 'She didn't want friendship. She wanted to be left alone.'

'Perhaps you only *thought* she wanted to be left alone.'

'No we didn't only *think* that! We tried. We were worried about her. She wasn't very robust and I think she was being . . . This is ridiculous. I mean I really don't know what went on. And I don't really know why I'm discussing it with you. We thought the obvious thing; that she was being beaten up by her lover. We

53

didn't think she was married because I noticed she never wore a ring.'

'Isn't it amazing what goes on in the name of keeping one's nose out of other people's business? If we stuck our noses in more often—'

'It sounds as though we were unsympathetic. We weren't. She as good as told us not to interfere.'

'I'm sorry. I didn't mean to imply anything.' Irene smiled. Linda felt the warmth. She felt the irritation begin to dissipate.

'It's not your fault,' Linda said. 'It's guilt, I suppose. We should have been able to do something. Anything . . .'

'Did you see the marks?'

'Of the beatings? Not really. On the few occasions I saw her in daylight close up her hair almost covered her face. You know it all happened in a short period. She was only here a couple of months.'

'And what happened in the end?'

'I'd already left for work when the ambulance came. Mr Leitman – he's a writer so he's home all day – he saw the ambulance.'

'I wonder who phoned for it.'

'Yes, we wondered too. Then we heard it was the milkman.'

'What a sad story. Do you think houses absorb sadness? Do you think they can communicate with you?'

Linda looked at her oddly. 'No, of course not. I'm sure you're going to be very happy here.'

'Are you?'

'Very. You'll forget about Grace soon.'

'I wonder.' She rose and went to the door. 'Do you think she could have been murdered?'

'Murdered! No, of course not. There was no suggestion of that. It was suicide. An overdose. It was all in the local paper.'

Irene smiled again. This time there was no warmth. It was chilly, forbidding. 'You don't want to believe everything you read in the papers,' she said.

At the time Macrae first joined the police, Battersea was much as it had always been, dismal. But over the years it had been gentrified. Except for small pockets. Macrae lived in one of these. At one end of his street the houses had been tarted up, at his end the front gardens had been concreted to make hard standing for cars, and what greenery was left was spindly and covered in grime. Variegated privet was the shrub of choice.

When Macrae got back to his small terraced villa it was empty. Frenchy had taken her bag and gone to work. The house was cold and smelled of stale cigar smoke, but before leaving she had tidied it up and washed the dishes and Macrae was grateful. He hated coming home to squalor but didn't do much about it.

He gave himself a whisky, looked at his mail – all bills or offers – and threw the lot in the bin. Then, still dressed in his hat and coat, he sat down at the kitchen table and pulled out his notebook.

ASSETS, he wrote at the top of a blank page. The enumeration of these took him five seconds: house, car.

The house carried a second mortgage and even if he put it on the market there was almost no chance, in the recession, of selling it. In fact his street was patterned with For Sale signs, some of which had been there for a year or more.

The car hardly existed in cash terms. No one would give him the time of day for it. It had a scrap value but that was about all.

LIABILITIES, he wrote.

Where to begin?

Abruptly he ripped out both pages, crumpled them up and threw them away.

To hell with liabilities.

The worst liability was Stoker. What really angered Macrae was that his dignity had been bruised even by having to speak to Stoker, by having to be in the same room with him. In the old days he would have knocked his teeth down his throat. Why hadn't he done so today? Was he himself getting old? Or was he gradually being sucked into the 'new' policing methods by fools like Scales?

Or was it none of these? Wasn't it simply the fact that if Stoker let it be known that he had borrowed money from a criminal acquaintance he'd be the subject of disciplinary proceedings the end of which might well mean having to leave the Force?

And did he want to leave the Force?

What would happen if he resigned? On the plus side the problem of Stoker would vanish.

What about money? He'd get a lump sum and a relatively small pension, so he'd need another job. He'd been offered several in private security at twice what he was getting in the police.

But he didn't want to work in private security.

He wanted to remain in the police.

He picked up the phone and dialled the *Chronicle* and asked for the chief crime reporter, Norman Paston.

'Hello, George. Got something for me?'

'Not this time.'

He could visualize Paston in his elegant 1950s tailoring, his yellow waistcoat, his handmade shirt, and his Sulka tie. A most unlikely figure to be rooting about in London's dirty washing but someone who rooted well and whose relationship with Macrae had lasted for years – on a strictly symbiotic basis.

'Remember Artie Gorman?' Macrae said.

'Vaguely.'

'Used to be a bookie's runner and then became legitimate. Made a lot of money.'

'Wasn't he mixed up in some betting fraud a few years back?'

'No one could prove it. Anyway, he died a few months ago and a villain called Stoker is living with his widow. Name mean anything?'

'Didn't he knife a copper?'

'Not a knife, a tyre lever.'

'What's the interest?'

'Molly – Artie's widow – has fallen for him, and he's playing about with her money. Pretending to be a financial expert when he can hardly sign his name.'

'So, I repeat, what's your interest?'

'I've always liked Molly and—'

'I see.'

'No, you don't see. It's not like that. I think he's going to bleed her white and dump her. And there's nothing I can do about it.'

'And you want me to keep my ear to the ground *vis-à-vis* Mr Stoker.'

'Aye. That's it.'

'Anything for you, Georgie.' His voice took on a voluptuously camp tone, one which he knew made Macrae sweat. 'We must get together. Come to lunch at the flat and bring that good-looking sergeant.'

'Silver? He's not for you, Norman. He's got a girlfriend.'

'If I had a ten-pound note every time I met someone who had a girlfriend and who—'

'Goodbye, Norman.'

Macrae put the phone down. Well that was a start. Paston had as good a nest of informants as he did and that was saying something.

He dialled Frenchy's ponce, Rambo. He had been one of Macrae's best sources of information for several years.

'Evening, Julius.'

Macrae was the only person, apart from his family, to call Rambo by his proper name.

'Evenin', Mr Macrae.'

'D'you know a villain called Stoker?'

At least he was doing *some*thing, Macrae thought.

8

She touched the walls with the tips of her fingers.

Had Grace touched these?

Did he who made the lamb make thee?

The line of Blake's, last read at school, flashed through her mind and tears came to her eyes.

No weakness!

It wasn't the first time she had said that to herself and wouldn't be the last.

She moved through the apartment, now with her own things in it. Did death leave an aura? Was there some shadow? A radioactive silhouette burnt on to the walls like those in Hiroshima?

I am a camera, she thought.

Yes? The man had said. Yes?

Yes.

Then he had flipped the sheet to cover Grace's face and pushed the sliding drawer back into the wall.

He was sorry. Was she all right? It was a shocking thing to have to do. Some fainted dead away.

Yes, she was all right.

In that case he needed her to fill in papers now, next of kin, identification, that sort of thing. And then there was the question of disposal.

Disposal.

The word brought bile into her mouth.

They left the big room with its smell of death and violent antiseptics and went to his office. She signed the papers.

She wanted Grace's things, she said.

After the inquest.

When would that be?

Soon. There were no suspicious circumstances so there would be no delay.

What about the letter? The one she had left.

Strictly speaking, it was one of Grace's effects.

For God's sake, she was—

Yes, he knew. He was merely trying to protect her. She could have a copy, if she wished.

She had taken the letter to her hotel room. She knew it was going to be terrible, and it was. In a way, even more terrible than the news of Grace's death.

There was no way she was going to read it cold. She had a bottle of gin and drank a double, neat. It gave her courage.

Mother (Not even 'Dear'. That had hit like
lightning, scorching her eyes. But what
had she expected?)

You must have entertained the possibility . . .

(Most began: By the time you read this I shall
be dead. But Grace was never ordinary.)

You must have entertained the possibility that
something like this would happen. I hope that you
care. I want you to care.

They say suicide is a search for blame and the paying
back of old scores. Children fantasize. Look what you
made me do, they say, you'll be sorry when you find
me dead.

Are you?

I tell myself the scenario. The phone call. Is that
Mrs Davies? This is the police. Do you have
a daughter called Grace? Yes? Then I'm sorry
to tell you—

Something like that.

*I see your face, frozen for a moment. And then you
hear the word 'overdose'. That is when I'd like to see
your eyes.*

*A thousand questions will go through your brain but
only one will matter. It is the question
all parents ask themselves. Where did I go wrong?*

*I'm going to leave you with that question. I wonder if
you will ever find an answer.
Grace.*

*Once she read it she knew why the man had tried to protect her.
She had drunk herself into insensibility that night, and every
night for weeks. It hadn't helped. She had to face it.
And she had faced it . . . Until the inquest. Until the medical
evidence of bruises, of battery. She felt the blows on her own flesh.*

Macrae had a few days of accumulated leave owing to him and
decided to take it. He had never been one for allowing things to
happen to him by chance. He had always gone out and taken life
by the throat and *made* things happen. The fact that life had often
retaliated by kicking him in the balls was something he had never
quite got used to.

Stoker came into this category. Macrae was damned if he was
simply going to sit back and wait for Stoker to do what he wanted.

But what *did* Stoker want, apart from the money? Six thousand
wasn't all that much when he was playing with Artie's fortune.
And it wasn't as though he was losing face because Macrae was
getting away with anything. It hadn't been his loan in the first
place. And anyway, no one knew.

So, if it wasn't the money, then what was it?

Macrae tried to recall in detail what had happened on the one
occasion he had had to deal with Stoker. He had been on loan to
Hackney to help them reorganize their area, when there was an
emergency call about the wounding of a local constable. He'd
been found unconscious and close to death. He had been struck
about the head – later they found the tyre lever – and his arm
had been broken.

Even though he was in severe pain he was able to identify his assailant and Macrae had gone out and brought him in. Stoker was seventeen then but a real villain, a throwback to the gangs of the 1950s. Macrae and two other officers had taken him down to the holding cells and dealt with him severely.

Severely meant loss of teeth, broken nose, two swollen eyes. Very severely would have meant some permanent damage. So in Macrae's opinion Stoker had got off relatively lightly when you combined that with being sentenced to youth custody. Macrae thought that people who stood on other people's arms and broke them did not really deserve much in the way of consideration.

But he was open-minded enough to accept that Stoker might have held a different view. It was possible he had not taken kindly to his beating and might have harboured a grudge against Macrae.

So . . . given all the circumstances, he could not see Stoker simply forgetting about the money just because he told him to get stuffed. Stoker was doing this to get his revenge, which would undoubtedly be sweet – if he managed it.

It wasn't often, Macrae thought, that tearaways like Stoker had such a strong position *vis-à-vis* a senior police officer. Twenty or thirty years ago it would not have mattered so much, things would have been hushed up. But now everything – or a lot of things – had to be done out in the open where the Great British Public could see and judge. And in the police force borrowing money from villains was especially frowned upon.

In which case Macrae was looking for a fall-back position.

But what?

He could try to fit Stoker up, but framing anyone needed the co-operation of other policemen. He considered Silver, his own partner, but there was no way he was going to involve him, he had too much pride for that. Anyway, he was never sure how Silver would react in a given situation – that was the problem of the highly educated intake of recent years: they thought too much.

And there was something else bothering him: how was he ever going to be certain – even if he managed to buy back the tape – that that was going to be the end of the story? Wouldn't Stoker simply produce another copy . . . and another . . ?

Information, that's what he needed, information which would

give him something as strong against Stoker as Stoker had against him. Then there would be a stand-off.

In which case there was no use sitting at home: the proper study of crime was criminals.

He decided to go on a tour of his manor and see how things stood, and what he discovered made him deeply uneasy. First he went to the Goodwood Sporting Club, which lay between the Strand and the Thames. It occupied the top two floors of a building in a small, twisting alley and its sporting ethos extended only to card games – mainly a form of gin rummy called kalooki, played for high stakes.

It was a club organized for criminals by criminals who liked to have somewhere they could display their 'wedges' – the thick piles of large-denomination banknotes kept together with silver clips – their Monte Cristo coronas, their Gucci this and Gucci that, in short somewhere they could go and have the simple pleasure of showing off their goods.

Macrae had used the Goodwood for years. He liked its dangerous atmosphere, he liked the slight frisson he felt when he mounted the stairs and walked into the gaming-room past the little statue of a jockey which stood near the door. But mostly he liked to see the expressions on the faces of the villains as he came in. They were usually mixtures of fear, hatred, and respect: no bad thing for a policeman, he always thought.

But on this January evening as he entered the room and walked past the gaming tables to the bar he felt a distinct difference in the atmosphere.

He nodded to one or two faces he had last seen in the dock at the Old Bailey but did not receive any recognition. He did not expect the really hard men to greet him; they resented his presence but were realistic enough to leave things as they were. But from the lesser fry, the pickpockets, the con artists, there would usually be a muttered, 'Evening, Mr Macrae.' Tonight no one greeted him. He might have been invisible.

'A pint and a dram,' he said to the barman, whose name was Freddy and who had been put away – not by Macrae – for helping old ladies over dangerous road junctions and leaving them with nothing in their handbags.

Freddy was polishing glasses as though his life depended on it.

His eyes were fixed on a point above Macrae's right shoulder.

In his time Macrae had ordered scores of pints from Freddy, now he appeared not to hear. Macrae repeated his order and a hush fell over the tables.

'Are you a member here, sir?'

'Of course I'm not a bloody member. What's the matter with you, Freddy?'

'Only members allowed to buy drinks at the bar, sir.'

'Since when?'

'Since today, sir. New rule of the club, sir.'

Slowly Macrae turned to face the room. He leaned back on the bar. There were half a dozen villains there who might have gone down for longer periods than they had done, except for deals made with him. Any one of them might have bought him a pint. No one moved.

Macrae slowly nodded his head. He wasn't going to demean himself by asking. If that's the way they wanted it, then fine. But why? Was something heavy in the wind? But this wasn't the sort of behaviour that presaged a major crime. Then everyone was nervous, jerky, and it was 'Evening, Mr Macrae . . . Evening, sir . . .'

And you could cut the tension with a knife.

Well, there was tension all right, but the wrong sort. No one was nervous. The tension had an ugly undercurrent to it.

Macrae moved away from the bar and picked his way towards the door. His back felt vulnerable. His hair prickled. The most violent man in the room was a stubby chunk of flesh and bone called Rubbers, who was playing cards at a table near the door. His head was completely bald and shone like a billiard ball. Macrae stopped at his side in an intense silence. He bent down and inspected Rubbers' bald dome and said, 'Coming along, nicely, laddie, just keep using the lotion.'

Then he went out and down the stairs.

It wasn't much, he told himself, but it was a gesture.

He visited a few pubs where known villains hung out. The atmosphere was the same and Macrae was a worried man when he reached his house. He had just finished frying himself a bit of bacon when the phone rang. It was Rambo.

'You got something good for me?'

'Well it is and it isn't, Mr Macrae.'

'Let's have it.'

'The word on the street is that a senior copper in Area One is bent.'

'What? Who?' He felt a cold hand close over his intestines.

'Well, that's the thing, Mr Macrae. I ain't got a name. Only that he was deep in the shit, owing money, that sort of thing.'

'OK, Julius, let me know if you hear anything further.'

'Count on me, Mr Macrae.'

He stood by the phone for some minutes. Then he poured himself a drink. In the kitchen the bacon grew cold and lay on a bed of white grease.

9

Manfred Silver, drying his plump white hands on a paper towel, entered the kitchen of his flat and stared broodingly at Zoe, who was standing over the stove stirring something he guessed was, in an hour or so, to be his dinner.

'What (*vot*) are you doing?' he said.

'Cooking.'

It was now nearly seven o'clock and Zoe had been in the kitchen since a little after six. There had been an office party for someone's birthday and she had had a couple . . . well, four . . . glasses of a fruity white wine from South Australia.

As she got out of the lift she could hear one of Manfred's pupils playing, very slowly, the Rondo alla Turka.

Manfred had heard the lift gates close and had put his head out of the music-room when she opened the front door.

'Oh, it's you,' he had said.

'Divino Mozartino,' she had replied.

'What?' The query contained irritation and bafflement but she was not about to try to explain Benson's Lucia to her common-law father-in-law. Shaking his head, he had gone back into the music-room and closed the door.

Now he approached the stove. 'Chicken,' he said.

'Chicken *marengo*,' Zoe replied.

'For marengo you use veal. My wife makes it so.'

'This is *chicken* marengo.'

'In Austria it is veal.'

'In Austria, if you'll forgive the word, it is pork. Or it was the last time I was there. Even the schnitzels were pork.'

So that the South Australian white should not be too lonely, Zoe had opened a bottle of red, had drunk two glasses, and was

65

floating slightly above the patterned linoleum floor.

'Would you like a glass of wine, Mr Silver?'

'Sure. Why not? What is it? French?'

'Spanish. From the Upper Ebro.'

'How do you know?'

'It says so on the label.'

'Oh.'

'How is Ruth?'

'Ruth is all right. A sore jaw, but she lives.'

'When do you think . . . you know . . . that Mrs Silver will come back?'

'God knows. Maybe never.' Zoe dropped a ladle with a clang. 'Maybe she likes it better there.'

She fed him chicken marengo, rice, and a green salad. He ate suspiciously.

'Aren't you eating?'

He said it as though she might have poisoned the food.

'I'll have mine when Leo gets back.'

'What is that?'

He poked something in the salad.

'Radicchio.'

'I don't like it.'

'OK. Just leave it.'

He munched on. Then he said, 'Leo was a good pianist when he was a little boy. God knows why he became a policeman.'

'It's just as well for me he did.'

She was referring to her persecution by a psychotic* during which time Leo had been her bulwark.

'He got stress from that last case.'

'I know.'

'Playing the piano is good for stress.'

'We couldn't get one into the flat. It's too small.'

'After you're married you can move to a bigger one here in North London near us.'

'What a good idea,' Zoe said, brightly.

Later, Manfred went to his chess club. Zoe did the dishes, then took her wine into the sitting-room. It was now after eight o'clock.

* *Thief Taker* by Alan Scholefield, Macmillan London 1991

She was used to Leo's erratic hours but didn't like them.

After you're married.

The phrase nagged at the edge of her mind. Did she want to get married? At one time she would have given her left arm to marry Leo. But now? Like father like son? Would marrying Leo mean marrying the Silvers? Would she, the only non-Jew among them, be swamped by this eccentric, restless, bickering family?

She heard the lift.

'Hi,' she said as Leo entered the room.

He didn't smile. His face was drawn; his eyes worried.

She cut off a smart remark, came over and kissed him, and said, 'Whatever it is it'll seem better after a drink.'

She gave him a glass of wine. He drained it and held out the glass. He wasn't much of a drinker so it was uncharacteristic of him and reminded her of the stress Manfred had mentioned. During that period he had drunk quite heavily but had seemed to get over it.

She came and sat beside him on the large sofa. 'Something's wrong. You want to talk about it?'

'Of course. Where's my father?'

'Chess.'

'OK. Well, Scales called me in to see him . . . that's why I'm late . . .'

Leo had been called to the deputy commander's office about six, just as he was going off duty.

'Sit down, Sergeant, make yourself comfortable.' He pointed to the red-and-white no-smoking sign on the wall behind his chair. 'You don't, do you?'

'Well, not regularly, sir.'

'Filthy habit. I'm trying to get rid of it throughout the station. Don't see why we should breathe other people's smoke, do you?'

Leo did not reply but he thought briefly that he wouldn't want to miss the encounter between Scales and Macrae when Scales asked him to stop smoking his thin cigars.

Scales was wearing a light-grey suit and had an array of pens in one of his waistcoat pockets. He took one out now, a spring-loaded ball-point, and began to click the point in and out. He went to the window and looked at the lights on the Embankment and the solid line of traffic.

'I've been watching you, Sergeant. And I like what I see.'

'Thank you, sir.'

'No need to thank me. It's me who should be thanking you. You're one of the new men, the men who are going to take the Met into the next century: young, educated, part of contemporary life.'

He turned. It was as though he was addressing a Rotary meeting, Leo thought.

'You know, Sergeant, for far too long the CID has acted like a posse in a Western. The form has been act first, ask questions later. Or I should say, *justify* those actions later. Know what I mean?'

'I think so, sir.'

Scales sat on his desk and stared down at Leo.

'It's been a bad couple of years for us. The worst I can remember, wrongful imprisonments, faked evidence, forensic uncertainties. The interesting thing, Sergeant, is that the men who faked the evidence are all senior officers. What does that tell you?'

Leo opened his mouth but Scales was in full flow. 'I'll tell you what it means: that the officers involved are from the old school, men who were moulded in the sixties and seventies, men who thought they were above the law . . . I hope you don't mind me speaking frankly to you like this.'

'No, sir.'

'Good . . . good . . . because it's unusual for a senior officer to discuss matters like this with a young sergeant. But that's part of how I see my job. Breaking moulds. That's why I need people like you on my side; young, intelligent, going places.' He paused. 'You *are* going places, aren't you, Sergeant?'

'I hope so, sir.'

'Well, you help me and I help you. That's the way it works.' He got up and strolled back to the window. 'You're Jewish, aren't you?'

'Yes, sir.'

'Not many of you in the Force. Don't think I've ever served with one before. I've always admired Jews, though. Clever people. Have you ever considered becoming a Mason? There's no . . . uh . . . restriction, you know.'

Leo allowed a small smile to touch his lips. 'No, sir, I hadn't.'

'Well, I should consider it if I were you, Sergeant. It helps, you know.'

'So I've heard, sir.'

'I'm sure I could find someone to propose you.'

'I'll think about it, sir.'

Leo thought of Macrae's face if this unlikely scenario ever took place.

'Excellent . . . excellent . . . Masonry has had a bad press recently, but it's a great force for good. Think of it in those terms, not just as a stepping-stone within the Force – although it is a very good one.'

Click . . . click . . . went the pen . . .

Scales said, 'I've thought about how best to use people like you. I want you to be my eyes and my ears. I'm stuck here with all this' – he waved at the paperwork on his desk – 'when I should be at the sharp end, out in the street, in a hands-on situation. Know what I mean?'

'Yes, sir.'

'But someone's got to mind the shop.' He smiled at this deprecating analogy. 'So I've come to depend on my private army. You could call it a force within the Force. People like yourself. And every now and then I need to ask someone in this private army to operate for me, discreetly. Someone I can trust. I *can* trust you, can't I, Leo?'

'Yes, sir.'

'Because when I say I should be out there in the street gathering information, it doesn't mean that I don't get *any*. I get quite a lot . . . quite a bit . . . '

Click went the pen.

'Something's come up, Leo, that needs looking into in the strictest confidence. And I particularly want you to be the one to operate. Do you think you could handle something in complete secrecy; I mean within the Force itself?'

'I'll do my best, sir.'

'Good man. It concerns Detective Superintendent Macrae.'

Leo felt his hands grow suddenly cold.

'There is word from . . . well, never mind where it's

from . . . that Detective Superintendent Macrae is in financial trouble and that he has accepted money from a known criminal. Do you know whether it's true or not?'

'No, sir, I don't, and I don't believe it either!'

'I'm not asking whether you believe it or not. Frankly, I don't *care* one way or the other. Your opinion is immaterial. Am I making myself clear, Sergeant?'

'Yes, sir, but—'

'Spare me your indignation. It isn't your loyalty to Macrae that interests me, but to the Force.'

'But, sir, I must just say one thing. I've worked with Mr Macrae very closely and—'

'Sergeant! If you don't know it already then you had better learn a basic truth – given the right circumstances, *anyone* can be corrupted.'

'Then, sir, the information is faulty. If you could tell me the source I—'

'We all have our private pipelines. I don't interfere with yours. Anyway, it doesn't matter where it came from, what matters . . . Look, don't get me wrong. I'm hoping you are going to prove it *false*.'

Leo's body had gone rigid with cold yet he was perspiring freely.

'I want you to report directly to me, Leo.' The voice was emollient once more. 'So that if and when your investigation clears him – as we hope it will – no harm will be done to him. I want it kept in the family, no matter what the outcome, and that wouldn't be the case if I called in the CIB and had a full-scale internal investigation. Are you with me?'

'Yes, sir.'

Leo finished telling his account of the interview to Zoe and they stared at each other in silence.

Then Zoe said, 'He's asking you to play Judas.'

'D'you think I don't know that!'

'Oh Leo, what a shitty thing to do. Did he really say "keep it in the family" and you're one of the "new men" and phrases like that? And anyway what's the CIB?'

'Complaints and Investigation Branch. And yes, he did.'

'And all this business about being a Freemason?'

'That too.'

'I thought Jews were barred.'

'No. That's not so. Apparently some Jews' best friends are Masons.'

'So what are you going to do?'

'God knows.'

'You'll have to tell Macrae, won't you?'

'Jesus, no. He'd probably get drunk and go in and have a row with Scales and abuse him and say things that he regretted. That's exactly what Scales would like. Then he's got him.'

'I don't suppose you can go to anyone else?'

'At Cannon Row? Not a chance. They'd say if Scales came to me on a job like this then I was his . . . his . . . '

'Creature?'

'That's as good a word as any.'

'So?'

'I'm in a cleft stick. I'm damned if I do and damned if I don't.'

'Leo, you don't think—? No.'

'What?'

'Well, you know it could, it just might, be true.'

She had feared he would explode at her; instead he swirled the last of the wine round and round the bottom of his glass.

He said, 'You don't know Macrae. He's a strange mixture. I mean I've seen him do things that make me wince. If he's convinced a villain is guilty he'll come down hard on him to get an admission. But I've never seen him take a bribe. I once saw someone offer him one and Macrae knocked him across a table and two chairs and if I hadn't stopped him he might have knocked him through a wall.'

'Didn't Scales say if the circumstances were right *no one* was immune?'

'Not Macrae. I'd bet money on it. I told you Scales talked about hands-on policing, well Macrae's a hands-on policeman. Some detectives sit and watch computer screens all day. Not Macrae. He can't stand computers. And he's not keen on the new policing methods. But he brings in the villains. That's the only reason I've stuck with him. He really hates them. And you wonder sometimes – or at least I do – what he'd do without them. It's like he's found his reason for existence. Like he's conducting a war, and he's

71

found the enemy, and he'd be lost without them. He *needs* them.'

'You really think you can judge Macrae?'

She had her hand on his arm and she felt him grow tense. She gave him half a glass of wine and poured a mouthful for herself.

She put her head against his shoulder. 'Of course you do.'

One of the problems of stress, she knew, was that people did not like to be contradicted.

'Look,' he said softly, 'I've told you what he's like when he gets drunk. I mean about not wanting me to leave him and all that. And how I've had to carry him into his house and put him to bed. Well, sometimes he talks about things, his childhood in Scotland for instance. His father was a bastard. He used to beat up Macrae's mother and Macrae himself when he was a kid. Macrae thinks all this came from humiliation.

'His father used to be a gamekeeper on a sporting estate in the Highlands and during the day he'd have to take a lot of shit from the wealthy sportsmen and say yes sir, no sir, three bags full, sir. So when he got home in the evenings he'd take it out on his family.'

'Didn't Macrae's mother kill herself?'

'They're not sure. She was found drowned in a salmon pool. You know, he likes to be ironic about my university background. But he also wanted to get a good education. He told me so. But his father said what the hell's the use of a good education on the moors?'

'Leo, what's all this got to do with Macrae taking or not taking money?'

'I'm trying to make you understand him. He wouldn't take money, not because of the moral side, he doesn't give a stuff about any morality except his own. No, he'd find it humiliating. I was on a bus with him once and the conductor hadn't been round to take the fares by the time we were getting off and Macrae didn't do what most of us would do, i.e., say, well, that's a nice free ride. No, he has to go and find the conductor and make him take the money. He hates being beholden to people. It's pride.'

'Which comes before a fall, as you'll remember.'

'Anyway Scales comes all this crap about hoping it's not true. Of course he's hoping it's true. But that's not the full story. At least I don't think it is. He's never liked Macrae, but that business

72

with Frenchy and Scales' mother really did it.'

'That was brilliant,' Zoe said.

He filled her in about Macrae's friendship with Artie Gorman and about Stoker and Molly and as he talked she felt him become stiffer and stiffer and saw perspiration on his brow. She wanted him to stop, to forget about it for a while, but he was talking more and more rapidly.

'But the other side is that if someone like Macrae goes down with a lot of publicity – which he would if the newspapers got hold of any whiff of an official internal inquiry – it would reflect badly on Scales. It's his patch. He's paranoid about keeping his nose clean. He's a bloody committee man. He's just a—'

'What about you, Leo?' She cut brutally over his jerky flow.

'What?'

'What if someone came and said here's fifty thousand pounds, just look the other way when I stick up yonder bank.'

He felt a hot flush of anger then looked at her eyes – and came down fast.

'Why fifty thousand? I'd do it for a fiver and a Big Mac. Oh, and by the way they don't say stick up a bank. Jesus Christ. Stick 'em up! What have you been watching?'

She had achieved what she wanted and put her arm round his neck. 'Leo, the sea-green incorruptible.'

Stress was not far from her mind – thanks to some music teachers she knew.

10

'You're Mrs—?' the receptionist said.

'Miss Isard,' Irene said.

'Oh yes, you've been here before, haven't you?'

'How's my mother?'

'Making progress.' The receptionist was a middle-aged black woman who wore a nurse's uniform and a severe expression.

'Dr Richards thinks she'll soon be ready to leave. That's if she has a place to go to.'

Irene said quickly, 'That's wonderful. We'll have to make plans.'

'Plans always help.' The tone was cynical. It suggested to Irene that this was a phrase she had heard many times before; that it was a metaphor for promises unfulfilled.

'Can I see her?'

'There's a singalong in the lounge but she never goes to those. Try the TV-room.'

Irene walked along a corridor that smelled strongly of antiseptic. Elderly patients (patient was a better word, Irene told herself, than inmate), some with walking frames, were shuffling down the long bright walkways. In the distance she could hear voices singing 'Abide With Me'.

Her mother was alone among the anonymous chairs of the TV-room. She sat at the opposite end to the set, which was on but with the sound turned down. She had her back to the room and was looking out of the second-floor window onto a small car park. Smoke rose from the cigarette in her hand.

'Hello, Mother.'

Mrs Isard did not react. She was in her early seventies but looked a hundred. She was wizened, a stick-figure – like a

74

Giacometti bronze, Irene thought – whose feet hardly touched the floor. She raised the cigarette to her mouth and Irene could see the yellow fingers and the tremor of her arm. Her eyes were half-closed against the smoke.

'I've brought you something.'

She gave her mother a package. It lay on her lap, unregarded.

'You can open it.'

She made no move.

Irene opened it. 'Peppermint creams. You like those.'

Mrs Isard pinched the end of her cigarette and put it carefully in a flat tobacco tin. Then she spoke. It sounded watery, like Portuguese.

'Put your teeth in, Mother.'

Teeth, covered in blood and tissue, on the kitchen lino. Her father, fist balled, standing over them.

Don't challenge him, her mother had always said. Never challenge him.

He waited. But neither challenged. Her mother couldn't, her jaw was broken. Irene didn't; she was learning fast.

That's where the teeth had gone. Her mother had been in her forties then. It wasn't nice to lose your teeth in your forties. Irene had only been a little girl.

Mrs Isard put her hand quickly to her mouth, made a small movement, and when she removed it her face had filled out substantially.

'You didn't come last week.'

The teeth clicked but at least Irene could make out the words.

'I told you, Mother, I was moving into a flat.'

'And that's more important!'

'I didn't say that. Of course you're important.'

'I'm used to it. You didn't visit me for years . . . and years . . . !'

Mrs Isard's fingers were working at the lid of the tobacco tin.

'Let me open it for you.'

'I can manage. I managed all those years without you.'

'I know that.' She didn't want to discuss this.

At last she got the lid off, selected a longish butt, and lit it.

75

'Please do not drop your butts in the urinal,' Mrs Isard said. 'It makes them soggy and difficult to light.'

Irene waited, she had heard it all before.

'Vic told me that. Told me he'd seen it written on the wall in a gents' lav.'

For a long time after his death Mrs Isard had not mentioned her late husband's name. It was as though she feared he might come up out of his grave and smash her face. But she had gradually become less afraid of him and because of that, Irene thought, he was being rehabilitated in her mind. One day she would no longer remember the broken bones, the missing teeth, and Vic would return to what he had originally been: the young man who had first made love to her, who had made her laugh with his jokes of soggy butts in the urinal.

'What are these?' Mrs Isard said.

'I told you. Peppermint creams.'

'I don't want the bloody things. You know what I want.'

'No, Mother, I do not know what you want.'

'Stuff. That's what I want.'

She knew but played it out. 'What sort of stuff?'

'Don't be stupid.'

'You said you'd been off it for years . . ! The last time—'

'Never mind the last time. If you were a proper daughter you'd think of me.'

'That's why I won't bring you drugs. That's exactly why. Because I *do* think of you.'

Over her mother's shoulder the silent set was showing a Tom and Jerry cartoon. The grey winter's day was closing down, the room was growing dark.

'How's your new room?' Irene asked. 'I'd like to see it sometime.'

'Why? Because you're paying for it? To see if you're getting your money's worth?'

'Not at all. Just seeing you safe and secure and comfortable is payment enough. Seeing you looked after like you should be.'

'It's a bloody institution! Don't you understand what that is!'

'I know it's a caring place.'

'Caring! It's a madhouse.'

'No it isn't. It's not that, Mother. It's a private nursing home.'

'It isn't, it's a loony bin.'

'Don't be so silly. It's what's called a half-way house.'

'Half-way to what? To Bedlam?'

'Where would you rather be? Here or that place where they found you the last time? Meths, for God's sake! And drugs and I don't know what. You were never like that.'

'How do you know what I was like? You weren't here! Anyway a daughter should look after her mother.'

'You know I couldn't.'

There was a pause.

Mrs Isard said, 'They say it would be better for me to live in the community. Who with, I asked, my daughter lives in Spain? They said Spain would be wonderful. Sun and oranges. And my own daughter. They wanted me to be with my family.'

'Stop it, Mother. There was no way. Carl was—'

'But I used to say she loves me very much. She writes to me all the time. But they knew I was lying. They do the post, you see.'

'Mother—'

'And every day I would say: Anything for me? And they would say: "No, Mrs Isard." But I wouldn't tell that to the others. I didn't want to be the only one without a letter.'

'All right! Get it all out! This is a kind of poison. You *knew* why we went to Spain. You *knew* Carl was ill. You *knew* I had to care for him.'

'He was a nancy boy!'

'He was kind and gentle!'

They stopped. In the sudden silence they realized they had been shouting at each other.

Slowly Mrs Isard put out her hand and Irene held it. 'Don't mind me. It's just—'

'I know.'

'I'm really very pleased to see you. You do know that, don't you?'

'Of course.'

She touched Irene's face. 'My daughter. My only daughter. Are you really here?'

'Yes, Mother, I'm really here.'

'Sometimes I can't quite believe it. Sorry . . . not about you being here. But about Gracie. I say to myself that it didn't . . . couldn't . . . happen. But it did, didn't it? It's not a dream, is it? Not part of all . . . all this . . ?'

'No, Mother, it happened. Grace killed herself and it's not part of a dream or your illness.'

'Last time you said murder.'

'That's my word for it. *They* called it suicide.'

'I should have done that,' Mrs Isard said. 'Then I wouldn't be in this place.'

'Please don't say that, Mother. I'm so glad you didn't. I have no one now. Carl's gone. Grace has gone—'

'There's only the two of us left.'

'Just the two of us.'

'Do you think, I mean . . . could we live together?'

'I've been thinking about it. Yes, we could. And I'll make it up to you, you'll see. I'll make it up for father and for Carl. We'll go away. Somewhere no one knows us.'

'That'll be lovely. Completely unknown.'

'That's right, by the sea perhaps.'

'I love the sea.'

'East Anglia.'

'Orford. Where I took you when you were little.'

'Somewhere like that. And we'll have a wooden house that looks out on the water and . . . Don't cry, Mother. Please don't cry.'

'But *when*?' Mrs Isard's voice was filled with pain. 'When?'

'Soon. I promise you it'll be soon. Just as soon as I find out about Grace.'

No man's land.

That's what Eddie always called it.

Gladys Twyford was standing at her sitting-room windows looking out at the exhausted grass and trees, the cracked concrete paths, the detritus, of the Green Leas Estate.

She could hear him now: 'Bloody no man's land out there. We're in a trench here and they're in a trench there, and that's no man's land. But they don't stay in their trenches. Bloody yobs.'

Not that Eddie had been in the war. Not the proper war. He'd been in Cyprus in the Emergency when he was doing his national service – but as a driver. Never with a gun, Eddie had always driven things.

That's what he had done in the police. It wasn't what he wanted to do. He'd wanted to be a detective but instead he'd got as far as a detective 'aide'. Not quite a detective but better than a copper on the beat. And then he'd been Mr Macrae's driver and that's what he'd liked best.

Gladys fetched her coat from the wardrobe. 'No good just standing here,' she said to bulldog. As she passed she touched his head for good luck. 'I'll go now it's quiet. Speak to Mr Geach. I'll tell him about the noise. The music. The bangings. He'll listen. It isn't as though I've got Eddie to protect me any more.'

Bulldog smiled at her. His pink tongue was hanging out and his head was on one side. He looked very like pictures she had seen of Sir Winston Churchill.

She began to plan her route. Mr Geach's office was in Jasmine House. That was two huge blocks away from her, beyond Primula and Marigold. A few years after they came to the estate Jasmine had been changed to Mandela House but was now Jasmine again. She didn't know why. She didn't know why it had been changed in the first place. Eddie had told her once but she had forgotten.

She had to walk about four hundred yards. It didn't sound much but it was through no man's land. She'd seen movies about the first war. Mines and snipers; bombs and guns; bayonets. It wasn't the Hun any longer but the young. Different enemy, but the same result.

'Just a coat,' she said to bulldog. 'No hat. I told you what happened last time when that kid knocked it off. Then he kicked it. God knows where it is now. And it was a good hat.'

But she needed something on her head because it was so cold. Yet a scarf . . . what if someone came up behind her, grabbed the scarf and twisted it round her neck . . . ? No . . . not a scarf.

Rape.

That was what she feared most.

There had been cases of elderly women raped in dim forgotten hallways.

It had bewildered her. 'Why women of my age?' she had said to Eddie. 'Why?'

'Perverts,' he had replied.

'I'll keep to the paths,' she said to bulldog. 'Stay away from the blocks.'

She took one last careful look out of the window. In the cold grey noon the estate was deserted.

'Right. I'm off.'

She locked and double-locked and triple-locked the doors. The wind was cold and she bent her body against it. She looked down at her feet as she walked.

'Don't have eye contact with anyone,' Eddie used to say.

That was the first time she heard the phrase. Now she knew she shouldn't have eye contact with people in pubs or shops or on buses or trains or on the streets. Only the other day she had looked up and seen a young man coming towards her in Battersea High Street.

'Get out of my way,' he said, and she'd had to step into the gutter.

When she'd been young she'd never walked with her head down. Then people looked at people. Nowadays if you looked someone in the eye you could be assaulted.

She passed Primula. A young person – she couldn't differentiate these days between male and female – was standing near the entrance. Gladys dropped her head and walked quickly past. At any moment she expected to hear a step, a voice, feel a push. She didn't have her bag. She had nothing of value. Her keys, on a piece of string round her neck, nestled between her breasts.

She felt her heart beat faster. Then she was clear of Primula and batting along towards Jasmine.

The notice on Mr Geach's door said Housing Manager. A few years back a secretary had sat just outside it, but she'd gone in one of the many cost-saving schemes. She knocked on the door.

'Yes?' The voice was displeased.

Timidly she opened the door. Mr Geach was seated behind his desk on which rested a mound of paper: letters, bills, estate notices, estate regulations. He was a plump man in his thirties, prematurely bald, with tufts of implanted hair growing out of small red scabs.

'Yes?'

'It's Mrs Twyford. Number Four, Rosemary.'

'Yes?'

He was holding one hand over the mouthpiece of his phone.

'If you're talking, I'll wait,' she said.

He looked at her angrily. 'What d'you want?'

'I come about the transfer.'

He opened his mouth as though to shout at her, then his expression changed.

He said into the mouthpiece, 'I've got to go now, Yvonne. No . . . No . . . Don't be like that. I'll talk to you later.'

Gladys heard a quacking noise come down the line then he replaced the receiver.

'Transfer? What transfer?'

'My husband, Mr Twyford, came to see you.'

'Twyford?'

'Mr Eddie Twyford.'

Geach shook his head. 'Don't remember him. I get a lot of people in here. Just because there's no one in now doesn't mean to say I don't get crowds.'

He got up from his desk and walked about the room. In one corner was a new set of golf clubs – the plastic wrappings still on the heads of the woods and irons. He took out a five-iron and waggled it in his hands.

'What d'you want a transfer for, Rosemary's all right isn't it?'

'It's terrible! I mean it's all young people. Not that I got anything against young people. We was all young once. But I'm not young, see. They have their ways and I have mine.'

'So you don't like youth?'

'No, sir, I never said that. I said—'

'What if everyone was your age? What would the world be like then?'

The phone rang. 'Yes? Oh, yeah. Tomorrow's OK. No . . . no . . . I can get away. First tee ten-thirty . . . Yeah. I got them . . . complete set . . . Mizuno.' He laughed. 'It's only money. Which reminds me . . . bring some.'

He put down the phone. Gladys said, 'It's the music. Thump . . . thump . . . thump . . . All night. I can't sleep. And they say they're selling drugs there. Banging on the doors all night.'

'Who says so?'

'Well . . . '

'That's a serious allegation, that is. It's a matter for the police. You should report it if you saw it.'

'I haven't *seen* anything. Nothing. No, no. But people talk . . . '

Geach looked at her severely, put the new five-iron back in the bag, pulled out a putter, and stroked a few imaginary balls.

'So where do you want to go if you got a transfer?'

'Somewhere it's quiet. Somewhere I'm not frightened all the time.'

He went to a big wall chart of the Green Leas Estate. Each block was broken up into squares with its number and the name of its occupants.

'Let's see . . . '

She waited. Hope soared.

He tapped the handle of the putter against the chart. 'Briar. You know Briar House?'

'It's the end one, isn't it?'

'That's it. Last block. Far away from Rosemary.'

'It's nearer the shops.'

'And the bus.'

'And the tube.'

'And it's mainly elderly people.'

It sounded like the Promised Land.

'Have you got a vacancy there?'

'No.'

'Oh.'

She felt dashed, as though he was playing a game with her.

'Not yet.'

Hope rose again. 'I could wait,' she said. 'If it wasn't long.'

'But . . . ' He tapped the chart again. 'Maybe . . . '

She felt she was being dangled over a cliff.

'There is one . . . no . . . '

'What?'

'I promised it to a lady in Marigold. But she's in hospital. They're not too hopeful about her coming out.'

'Mr Geach, I—'

'They're not sure.'

'But couldn't you—?'

'Wouldn't be fair, would it? She comes out and there's no flat. That's not right.'

No, she thought, it wasn't right. What if it was her coming out of hospital and the flat was gone, the flat she was looking forward to? She remained silent.

He hit the chart a good whack with the putter. 'But time and tide, Mrs . . . '

'Twyford.'

'Time and tide wait for no man, Mrs Twyford. Anyway she hasn't paid the admin costs.'

'What's that?'

'Administration costs.'

'Costs?'

He smiled at her. 'All this costs money, you know.'

'But I thought the council—'

'They *used* to pay the admin costs. But now we've got to find the money ourselves. It's what Mrs Thatcher wanted us to do. Be self-sufficient. Stand on our own feet.'

'How much are the administration costs?'

'Five hundred pounds.'

'Five hundred!' She was shaken.

'And in cash. The authorities like it in cash. Safer than cheques.'

'But I've only got Mr Twyford's pension.'

'Depends how much you want to move, doesn't it?'

The phone rang. 'Yvonne? Yeah. Right. Hang on a sec.' He covered the mouthpiece of the receiver with his hand. 'Think about it, Mrs Twyford.'

Still bewildered, Gladys went out into no man's land. At first she thought all was quiet. Then, out of the mist, came a line of youths. Six or eight of them, dark shapes in the swirling fog.

Afraid, she backed into the doorway.

But they did not see her. They went on in silence, a group yet not a group, marching . . . marching . . .

11

'It was my mother's business,' Gerald said. 'I joined her after I left school.'

'Let me get you another drink,' Irene said.

As she moved to take the glass from him there was a low rumble in the dog's throat.

'It's all right, old chap,' Gerald said, patting him.

He had come half an hour earlier – at Irene's request – to make an inventory of dilapidations to accompany the lease of the flat. She had seen him arrive in a black Porsche Carrera. At first she thought it was being driven by an animal. A huge tan-coloured dog was sitting in the passenger's seat in its own safety harness. The dog's name was Simba and Gerald had brought him in on a stainless-steel choke-collar. The leash was plaited leather and looked expensive. Simba was now lying alert on the floor at Gerald's feet. His size made the room look small.

'I've never seen a dog like that,' Irene had said as they entered the flat.

Simba was obviously a talking point and Gerald spoke about him over the first drink.

'He's a Ridgeback. They were used for hunting lions in Africa at one time. There's the ridge.'

He ran his finger along the ridge of hair which lay along the dog's spine.

'He's beautiful,' she said.

'Best dog in the world. Anyone lay a finger on me he'd have his arm off. But gentle with kids, aren't you, old chap?'

As he spoke she watched him. He was wearing cowboy boots with high heels and designer jeans. With his fair skin and blond moustache he gave the impression of being a kind of albino Swedish cowboy.

'Nice,' he said, indicating the furnishings.

'I used to live in Spain.'

The room was a mixture of the hot reds and yellows of a bullfighter's cape.

'I went there a couple of times to shoot partridges. It's ruined now.'

'There are still unspoilt places.'

'Not that I found.'

She did not want to argue about Spain. She felt defensive about it. Instead she asked him about the estate agency business. Wasn't it doing badly in the recession?

Not really. He'd seen it coming and gone heavily into the rental side. So when the selling market went into meltdown he had a large number of rental properties on his books. In a property recession people rented.

'That was lucky,' she said.

'I wouldn't call it luck.' His tone was flat.

'No, of course not. Forward planning.' She smiled her all-embracing smile. 'Isn't there a Marshall? Marshall and Masters?'

'Old Marshall started the agency in the fifties. It wasn't much. Specialized in small shops and down-market properties. When the housing market boomed he couldn't cope. My mother was working for another agency. She saw what was coming and went to him with a deal.'

'So Marshall and Masters was born.'

'It should really be just Masters now. He was supposed to retire a year ago. But he comes into the office all the time. Can't keep away. So I've let him have a desk and he does odds and ends.'

'What about your father?' she said.

'He died when I was a child.'

She waited for him to continue but he remained silent and instead leaned forward and began fondling the dog's ears.

This was sticky, she thought, and decided she would get on with discussing the dilapidations after he had finished his drink.

She felt him studying her. She was wearing a long dark red kaftan with gold strappy sandals. She knew she looked good.

'I like your car,' she said.

He glanced up quickly. 'You know about cars?'

'A little.'

'What d'you drive?'

'Oh, nothing. Small . . . French. I've always admired Porsches.'

'I wanted one ever since I was . . . I don't know, about twelve or thirteen, I suppose.'

'It was an amazing sight.'

'What?'

'Simba sitting in the front seat.'

'Where I go he goes. Except the woods. Isn't that right, old chap?'

He was waiting for her to ask why, and she did so.

He said he liked to hunt deer in thick woods. He had this friend in Hampshire with a thousand acres of dense woodland full of fat roe deer. He talked about hunting and she gave him another drink. He settled back in his chair, a faint flush on his face.

Thick woodland was the only place to hunt, he said. You gave the animal as much chance – more, in fact – than you had yourself.

But wasn't hunting, well . . . ?

He knew what she was going to say. Did she eat meat? Then she was simply shifting the responsibility for killing on to someone else's shoulders. It was killing by proxy.

That was an interesting phrase, she said. Killing by proxy. She wondered if it applied to the young woman who had occupied the flat before her.

How? It was suicide. Said so in the papers.

But it was caused by *something* or *someone*. It didn't just happen.

Oh, yes, it did. It was called 'while the balance of the mind was disturbed'.

With all those bruises on her body it would have been surprising if the balance *hadn't* been disturbed, didn't he think?

He shrugged. 'Shall we do the inventory?' he said.

He followed her round with a small notebook. The dog sat and watched. She was very aware of his closeness.

'Did you know her?' she said.

'I rented the place to her. Took her out to lunch a couple of times.'

'Grace.'

'That's right. How do you know?'

'Junk mail. Miss Grace Davies. It still comes.'

'You'd better let me have any post.'

'Why?'

'I'll send it on.'

'Who to?'

'She had a grandmother. I think she gave me her address once.'

They discussed a damp area below the kitchen sink. He made notes.

Then she said, 'What was she like?'

He stared at her. 'Why are you so interested?'

'I live in her aura.'

He blinked. 'Aura?'

'Can't you feel it?'

'No. If that's the lot I should be going. Thanks for the drinks.'

At the door she said, 'Can I pat Simba?'

'Sure. Just move slowly.'

'Good boy.' She scratched Simba's head.

'You'll need to sign the inventory,' he said.

'I'll drop by the agency.'

She went to the pavement, saw him strap the dog into the car. He leaned over the roof. 'You're not married, are you?'

'Was.'

'Would you like to go out to dinner sometime?'

'Why don't you give me a call?'

'OK, I'll do that. Ciao.'

Then he started the car and the powerful engine rumbled off down the street.

The village was in darkest Suffolk. Leo Silver found it after becoming lost three times and backtracking twice. He had left the main road in broad daylight but by the time he reached Lupton the roads had given way to lanes and finally the lanes to tracks.

Eddie Twyford would have hated this, he thought, as the Golf slithered through yet another long, muddy pool. Eddie had never really got on with the countryside.

Lupton had no proper centre, no pub, no church, no green, no ducking pond, indeed nothing that picturesque villages were supposed to have. It was bloody awful, Leo thought. He stopped at a gingerbread cottage and asked the way. As he waited he half expected a forest troll to answer his knock, but an ordinary housewife – reassuring – pointed the way to Hanger Lane.

The cottage stood by itself near the edge of a muddy track. Its curtains were half drawn and the light was like a beacon in the growing darkness.

Leo pushed open the gate and went up the narrow brick-lined path. A young woman with a baby on her arm came to the door.

'Are you lost?' she said.

'I don't think so. Are you Mrs Waddell?'

She frowned, suddenly wary. 'Why?'

'I'm looking for Ken.'

'Why?'

'Mum!' A child's voice came from upstairs. 'Mum! I've got soap in my eyes.'

'I'm coming, Stephen. Why do you want Ken?'

'I just want to ask him a couple of questions.'

'Mum!'

'What about?'

'About someone he once knew. I'm a police officer from London.' He showed her his warrant card.

'You don't look like a copper.' Her tone was hostile.

The baby began to sniffle.

'Can I see Ken?'

'He isn't in from work yet.'

'Mum!' It was a shriek.

'Oh God. All right! I'm coming! You'd better come in. He'll be home any minute now.'

She had been standing with the light behind her and he was able to see her more clearly when he entered. She was pale and thin and wore a jersey, skirt, slippers, and an apron.

'I'm trying to get the kids done before Ken comes home.' Her accent was south-east London and he imagined she had grown up on one of the housing estates like Green Leas. Well, she was in the green and muddy leas now and he wondered how she liked it.

The cottage was two up and two down but the ground floor had been knocked into one big open-plan room. There was a sitting area and a kitchen/dining area.

'Sit down while I see to Stephen.'

Stephen, with soap in his eyes in the bath upstairs, had begun a screeching wail that set Leo's teeth on edge. His list suddenly expanded: no coffin burials, no living on estates – and no kids. But he wouldn't tell Zoe. Not that she ever talked about kids. But sometimes there was a broody look about her when he mentioned his little nephew, Stanley. In fact he liked Stanley. Very much. But not too frequently.

He looked round for somewhere to sit. The three-piece suite was a bilious green and there were stains of dubious origin. So he perched on a corner of the kitchen table while he listened to Stephen being calmed down.

Then he heard the steady thump, thump, of a powerful motorcycle engine and through the window saw a man come into the back yard on a mud-spattered Honda ATV three-wheeler.

Ken Waddell was a big man with a big square face. Leo introduced himself while Waddell washed his hands in the kitchen sink.

'Mud,' he said, letting out the brown water. 'Hardly knew what it was when I lived in London, now it's like a second skin.'

'Are you farming?' Leo asked.

'God no. I couldn't afford land. No, I'm keepering. Learning to anyway. Chap here's got a pheasant shoot. That's what I've been doing today, putting the pegs in for tomorrow's shoot and feeding the birds.'

'The condemned pheasant ate a hearty meal,' Leo said.

Waddell smiled dutifully as he dried himself on a towel that had gone grey. Leo watched his hands and arms.

'What's it all about, then?' Waddell said. 'Don't believe we've had a visit from the Met down here. Not since I retired.'

They sat facing each other on the bilious green moquette. Waddell made no effort to put Leo at ease. He wasn't hostile as his wife was but he wasn't friendly either.

'Stoker,' Leo said.

'Oh, Christ.'

'Sorry.'

'What's he been up to this time?'

'Well, that's it. We think he's involved with a senior officer in the Met.'

'D'you mean sexually involved?'

'God, no!' Leo had a sudden vision of Macrae and Stoker in each other's arms. 'No, no, the usual. Backhanders.'

'What? Stoker? You must be joking! That shit's never had two pennies to rub together. Where's he going to get enough bread to bribe a senior officer?'

'I'll tell you if you'll answer a couple of questions first.'

Waddell had brought an agricultural air with him compounded of mud, manure, and animal feedstuff. Leo thought the word might be 'ripe'.

'I'll try. But it was a few years back.'

Leo got him to repeat what had happened to him the night he was injured. He told it briefly, in clipped sentences, as though giving evidence in court.

While he was speaking his wife came down the stairs and began clearing up the mess her husband had made at the sink.

Suddenly she cut across the conversation. 'Why are you bringing all this up again? Why don't you leave us alone?'

'Forget it, Trudy love,' Waddell said.

'Forget it? That's all you ever say about anything. Leave it! Forget it! They trampled all over you, the police did. Now you say forget it!'

She turned to Leo. 'I don't know what you want with Ken but you've no right to ask him anything, no right to expect any co-operation after what your people did to him.'

'Trudy!'

'I *will* speak. I've never said anything to anybody in the Force, not all this time. But I'm really disgusted. We both are, only Ken won't say all he feels. Three years! That's all that bastard Stoker got. And then it was soft time.'

'He was only seventeen,' Waddell said. 'Youth custody.'

'Three years for breaking Ken's arm and smashing him with a tyre lever.'

'It was my own fault really, I—'

'Don't go on saying that!'

'Well, it was. Here was this young bugger piling things into a car at three o'clock in the morning. And when I questioned him he said he and his girlfriend had had a row and she had kicked him out and made him take his belongings. It was possible, you know. Things like that happen. But even so I thought I'd have a bit of a look. He had a painting and some silver and a couple of stereos. Not his sort of gear. Anyway, before I could say anything he came at me.

'You know as well as I do we're trained not to do that sort of thing if we're by ourselves. I should have radioed for backup, that's what I should have done.'

'By the book,' Leo said.

'Yeah, I should've done it by the book.'

His wife laughed harshly. 'That's what they did to you. They stuck you with the book. Look at that arm. Nothing the matter with it. He uses it all day . . . '

'That's true,' Waddell said. 'It took a long time to heal but it's OK now.'

'But when it mended they'd only offer him clerking. For someone like Ken!'

'I always wanted to be a beat copper,' Waddell said, 'ever since I was a little kid.'

'It's the only thing that made him happy. Now look what's happened. Stuck in this mud trap. I don't see a living soul from one day to the next.'

'It's worse for her,' Waddell said. 'She has the kids all day.'

'And what about you?' Leo asked.

'It's not too bad. I'm out of doors. It's just that I miss the lads in the canteen and in the pub after coming off shift. You know, taking the mickey. And I miss London too. Sometimes I think . . . well . . . doesn't matter now what I think, does it . . . ? So . . . Your turn.'

Leo had thought carefully on the way down how he would tell his story. Keep it simple, brief, and don't lie too much. But it had to be believable. Waddell was no fool. So he told him the truth or as much of it as he could. He didn't give any names though and placed it in a different Area.

'Why don't you leave it to the CIB, that's their job, isn't it?'

'Because he's the best thief taker we've got. Anyway I don't believe most of it. That's why I came to see you. Anything you can tell me about Stoker might help. I mean anything you might have known that wasn't on his record.'

'What you're saying is you'll blackmail him into shutting his face.'

'Something like that.'

As he said it Leo realized he was about to cross a line. He hadn't yet but that's what he was indicating he was going to do. It was what Macrae would have done. And Leo would have felt contempt for the method. But, he told himself, he didn't *have* to do it. It was only talk at this stage. But he knew Waddell was right. If he did get the information he probably would. Probably . . . possibly . . . he hung on to their vagueness . . .

'You didn't tell me where Stoker got the money from. Isn't that where you'd look first to find dirt?'

'We know. And it doesn't help.' He told Waddell about Artie Gorman and Molly.

'The bookie?'

'That's him.'

'I remember Honest Arthur Gorman, the punter's friend. He had a betting shop in Camden.'

'He had a chain of betting shops in north London.'

'Yeah. There was something . . . ' He paused, thinking.

'What?'

'Well, it was just before I resigned. I was doing a turn in Camden. Records clerk. Anyway, they found this body on Primrose Hill. A nasty piece of work called . . . what the hell was his name? A bird. Sparrow or Pigeon, Thrush . . . no not thrush . . . I've had thrush . . . Anyway, a bird's name. He'd been battered about the head. They found a tyre lever not too far away, hidden in a holly hedge.'

'That's why you remember. The tyre lever.'

'Exactly. No prints, unfortunately. The word was that this bloke with a bird's name had got this hands on a lot of bread from a bullion robbery and used it to start gambling operations in Gorman's patch and Gorman warned him several times and then got someone to give him a stern talking to – just break his arm or a couple of fingers – something like that. But the someone went too far. There were people, me included, who thought that the someone was Stoker.'

12

Macrae stood on the step and pressed the doorbell.

Mandy Parrish, once the second Mrs Macrae, opened the door as though he was expected.

'George? What are you doing here?'

'I was passing.'

She was wearing a long salmon-pink housecoat – or maybe it was a dressing-gown, he thought. She smelled as though she had just come out of a bath. She was in her thirties, fleshy, with thick black hair and dark eyes that promised things you never read about in books. And, in Macrae's experience, delivered some of them.

'You look good,' he said.

'Thank you.'

'Thought I'd look in and see how you were. Say hello to the kids.'

'It's ten o'clock in the morning, George. The kids are at school.'

'It's half-term, isn't it?'

'In January? They've only just started the new term. Anyway, you get them next weekend.'

'Aren't you going to ask me in?'

She looked briefly at her watch. 'It'll have to be just for a minute. Then I've got an appointment with my osteo.'

He had only been in the house once or twice. Usually, when he brought the kids back after an outing, he said goodbye to them in the car.

It was a small semi-detached house in an area of London which had been badly bombed during the war. Many of the new buildings had been built in the 1960s in the stained concrete style of the times which made even brown stucco look good.

He thought she wasn't overwhelmed to see him.

She took him into the living-room which was all shiny veneer and new horse brasses.

'How're you keeping?' he said. It sounded false, as though he was talking to someone's aunt and she didn't bother to reply.

'Passing where to?' she said.

'Just passing. I've got a few days off.'

'And?'

'And what?'

'You thought why not go and see Mandy.'

'You should be flattered.'

He waited to be offered a coffee but the question was not raised.

'I am, George, I am.'

There was a fake ormolu clock on the fake mantelpiece. She glanced at it. It was showing 10.08.

'How's Joe?'

'He's fine. He's gone to work.'

'How's he doing?'

'For God's sake, George, what do you care how he's doing? Oh! Listen, if you've come to see if you can get me to reduce the maintenance payments for the kids forget it.'

'I told you why I came.'

'You've always been a rotten liar.'

'Aye, that's a fact. All right, I came because I knew Joe would be at work. I came because I thought you and I—'

'You randy old bugger!'

'Lassie, you always do it to me.'

'Well, it's got to stop. It's not fair on Joe, is it?'

'Joe's got you all the rest of the time. Anyway, how's he doing?'

'You just asked that. Why're you so interested? You've never given a stuff about Joe before.'

'Well, I mean . . . looking around . . . everything seems nice . . .'

'Joe's doing OK. He works hard. He wants to give me nice things.'

'Has he still got three cabs?'

'George, what the hell has Joe's financial affairs got to do with anything?'

'I'd like to have a word with him about something.'

'So it isn't a quickie with the ex-wife. I don't know whether to feel insulted or pleased. I suppose you've still got that tart Frenchy hanging about.'

'She's a good friend to me.'

'I never thought you'd have to buy it, George.'

'That's not the case at all.'

'What's this something you want to have a word with Joe about?'

'A business proposition.'

She laughed, unamused. 'Business proposition! You? Come on, George. You wouldn't know a business proposition if you fell over one. Not unless . . . George, you're not in trouble are you? Is that it? I mean this whole thing, the visit, just passing—'

There was a crash as the front door burst open. Joe Parrish, taxi driver and master of the house, stood on the threshold. He looked at Macrae and seemed stunned for a moment.

'You! Christ, I never thought it was you!'

'Joe!' Mandy's voice was like a whip.

He planted himself in front of Macrae. He was inches shorter.

'Joe! Don't be stupid.'

Usually he did what Mandy told him to do. This time he didn't. 'Shut up!' he shouted.

'Don't you tell me to shut up!' She grabbed his arm and turned him towards her.

He slapped her hard in the face.

'Oh!'

The unexpectedness of it as much as the blow caused her to drop into a chair holding her cheek.

Macrae said, 'Joe! This isn't what you think. I was passing and—'

'You bloody liar. You've been having it off with my wife in my house in my bed. You bastard!'

'That's not true, laddie. If you want to know the truth it was you I came to see.'

'Bollocks! There's something going on here. I've known about it for weeks. That's why I came back.'

'You rotten little bugger!' Mandy pushed herself up out of the chair. 'Sneaking. That's what you are, a sneak!'

96

'You want another?' Joe shouted. 'You're going the right way about it.'

That seemed to exhaust them for a moment and they stared at each other in silence.

Macrae said, 'Joe, I swear to you—'

'Who's that?' Joe said. There was the sound of a car engine idling outside the front door. Joe turned to the window. Macrae caught a sudden look of apprehension in Mandy's eyes.

Joe ran down the passage to the front door. There was a squeal of tyres and the car accelerated down the street.

Mandy said to Macrae, 'A fine mess you've made of this, George.'

'Don't be bloody silly. He might have caught you in bed. As it is he won't be sure now.'

Joe returned. His face was bloodless.

'Well?' Mandy said, seizing the initiative. 'What're you accusing me of now?'

Joe was genuinely bewildered. 'If it's not George it's someone else. I'm bloody positive.'

'Just anybody, is it? Anybody who stops his car near the house. You're going barmy, Joe.'

'Aye,' Macrae said. 'You'll have a breakdown if you go on like this.'

Joe sat down and put his face in his hands. 'I could have sworn. I . . . Maybe it's being alone in the cab all day.'

'Too much time to think,' Macrae said.

'And maybe you should apologize to both of us,' Mandy said. 'You want some coffee, George?'

But the purpose of Macrae's visit was damaged beyond repair. 'No thanks. I'll be off. Take it easy, Joe. Remember *Othello*.'

Joe and Mandy stared uncomprehendingly at him as he went out into the street.

Irene stood at the door of her mother's room and, unnoticed, watched her for a moment. Mrs Isard was sitting upright on the edge of her bed, hands folded in her lap, staring straight ahead as though she was blind. She looked so small and frail that for a moment Irene felt her throat close with emotion. She shouldn't look like this, she thought, not in her seventies. It was unfair.

'Have you been waiting long?' Irene crossed the room and kissed her.

'Since half-past nine.'

It was now half-past eleven.

'We're going out for lunch, Mother, not breakfast.' It was meant as a joke, but Mrs Isard did not smile.

'Have you got everything? Do you need to go?'

'No thank you.' Her mother's expression became irritated.

'It's sunny. What about the country?'

'I don't mind where we go as long as it's out of this bloody place.'

Irene took her arm as they went along the corridor. Lift doors clanged. Old people shuffled in and out.

'Going up?' a voice said.

'Down,' Irene said.

They waited.

'The more senile you get the higher you go,' Mrs Isard said. 'When you reach the sixth floor that's the end. You're finished then. You'd think they'd do it the other way; start at the top and work down to the basement. That's where the incinerators are.'

'You'll be out of here soon, Mother, I promise you.'

They drove into the Thames valley, the sunshine was bright, the morning frosty. They stopped near Marlow at a pub on the river.

'It's in the Guide,' Irene said. 'The food's supposed to be good.'

The pub restaurant was rather smart. They were seated at a window. The river was below them. A couple of narrowboats were moored on the far side. A pair of swans drifted by.

They ordered sole. Mrs Isard had always liked Dover sole. Irene worried about the bones.

'Would you like me to ask them to take it off the bone?'

'I can manage.'

A waiter appeared and asked if they'd like to see the wine list.

'No thanks—' Irene began.

'I'd like some wine,' Mrs Isard said. 'White wine with fish.'

'Do you think you should, Mother? You know how it—'

'I'd like a glass of white wine.' Mrs Isard was firm.

Irene ordered two.

'I'm not an alcoholic,' Mrs Isard said when the waiter had gone.

'I didn't say that.'

'But you think it.'

'It's just that it makes you . . . you know. Do you want to go?'

'No, I don't.'

Mrs Isard picked at her sole. The bones got in her teeth and she left most of it.

'Would you like something else? A sweet from the trolley? An ice cream?'

'I'd like another glass of wine.'

'I don't think that would be wise. And Mother, please, not that old tin.'

Mrs Isard had taken out her old tobacco tin and was selecting a half-smoked butt.

'Let me get you a proper packet.'

She ordered a packet of cigarettes and her mother lit up.

'Your father used to smoke these.'

Irene remembered the picture of the bearded sailor on the packet.

They settled back with their coffee. Mrs Isard seemed to have forgotten about ordering the second glass of wine. She smoked and looked at the swans.

'When you were little I used to take you to see the ducks in Battersea Park.'

Irene had a fleeting memory of mud and bits of soggy white bread floating on the filthy water. The ducks had been too bloated with food to eat her offerings.

'I used to take Grace to the Serpentine,' Irene said. Then, 'I spoke to the milkman.'

'What milkman?'

'I told you. She was found by her milkman. He said he'd hardly ever seen her. But he'd heard her typing.'

'Typing?'

'That's what he said. Maybe it was secretarial work.'

'Where did she get the money to live?' Mrs Isard said. 'That's what I'd like to know.'

'I sent it to her bank. It was Carl's really.'

'Blood money! Guilt money!'

'Not so loud, Mother!'

'You ignored us, Grace *and* me.'

'Please . . . not now. Don't you want to know about the milk-man? He said she owed him for three weeks. That's why he went round the side of the house. He saw her through the window.'

'I saw your father look through a window at me once.'

'Where was that?'

'At the refuge. I'm thirsty.' She caught the waiter's eye. 'Bring me a brandy. A large one.'

'Yes, madam.'

'Mother. Why not—'

But the waiter had gone.

'You didn't like the refuge, did you?'

The people at the nearest table paid their bill and left and Irene was able to relax slightly.

'No, I didn't. Nor did the other kids.'

'It saved my life – and yours. Vic would have killed me in the end. Or I would have killed myself.'

She drank half the brandy in a gulp.

'You nearly did anyway. Later, I mean.'

'Don't be impertinent. It was my life.'

'I was part of it. You forgot that sometimes.'

'Oh, so I'm to blame, am I?'

'I'm not apportioning blame. It just happened.'

Mrs Isard finished her brandy and looked round for the waiter.

'No more, Mother. That's it!'

But Mrs Isard was not to be balked. 'If you don't order me another I'm going to piddle on the chair.'

'Don't you dare. Do you want to go?'

'No, I don't want to go. For God's sake stop treating me like a child. Just order me the brandy.'

'Mother, listen to me. If you don't behave I'm going. I'm leaving you here. Don't think I won't. And you can find your own bloody way back.'

Mrs Isard looked at her, a calculating expression in her eyes. 'You would, wouldn't you? You left me before.'

'That's right. Now go to the loo and I'll order you another brandy. A small one. OK?'

Mrs Isard rose. Irene rose with her, spoke to a waiter, physically turned her mother in the direction of the ladies' toilets, and watched her totter off. She had a sudden and overpowering desire

to flee the place and never see the old woman again. But she
went back to the table.

*It was true about Vic. He would have killed her mother. And Irene
too. His drinking had been getting worse and worse.*

*Irene had written a letter. She would never forget some of the
words. They were an epigraph to her mother's life.*

*Vic had thrown boiling water at her mother. She could not use
her right arm. Irene was a teenager at the time. They had read
about Women At Risk. Irene had written to them in her mother's
voice.*

*I have spoken to my lawyer. He knows my husband's terrible
record for violence. He says that until he actually kills me, or
seriously injures me, nothing can be done.*

Actually kills me.

She remembered that phrase best of all.

And it wasn't for want of trying.

*He'd hit her with bricks and fists, he'd kicked her. He'd smashed
a glass in her face. He'd thrown her from a moving car.*

And the teeth. She remembered those. On the kitchen floor.

*So one night, when he was out drinking, they'd left. Just taken
a few things in a suitcase, and caught the Underground to Hammer-
smith and knocked on the door of the refuge.*

I wrote you a letter, her mother had said. Come in, they said.

For the first time in her life Irene did not feel afraid.

It took her mother longer. Vic would find them, she had said.

And he had.

He'd looked at them through the window.

I want my wife and child, he'd said.

*But the other women would not let him. They're ill, they said.
Sick. Go away.*

*He'd smashed the gate, but he'd gone. Irene never saw him
again.*

'Excuse me, madam. The lady with you . . . '

Irene came hurtling back to the present like a missile from its
silo.

'What?'

'The elderly lady . . . '

'What's happened? Has she had a fall?'

She followed the waiter through the restaurant. Her mother was in the bar draining the last of a glass of brandy.

'Mother!'

Mrs Isard turned slowly.

'How many has she had?'

'That's the second at the bar, madam'.

'My daughter will pay,' Mrs Isard made an expansive gesture with her arm that almost unbalanced her. She steadied herself on a bar stool. 'I do not carry money. Will you take a cheque? Makes no difference, they don't let me have a cheque-book.'

The young barman was looking apprehensive.

Mrs Isard held on to the bar stool. 'Can I have another?'

'No you can't. We're going.'

Mrs Isard went down on her knees and embraced the bar stool. 'I don't want to go!'

Irene paid the bill.

'Mother, you're making a scene.'

She took her mother's arm but Mrs Isard clung on to the bar stool.

'Can you help me?' Irene said to the waiter.

Mrs Isard began to weep.

'Prise her fingers off,' Irene said.

They managed to get the stool away from her mother.

'Let me, madam. She's only a little thing.'

The waiter picked Mrs Isard up as he might a small child and carried her out of the pub to the car park. Between them they managed to get her into the car with the seat-belt fastened.

'A strait-jacket!' Mrs Isard plucked at the seat-belt. 'Just like the hospital.'

Irene gave the waiter a fiver and thanked him.

'Not at all madam, I had a grandmother who liked brandy.'

Mrs Isard slept all the way back to London.

13

'Leo, you've got to do something!'

'What can I do?'

'Don't ask me. It's your family.'

'I know,' he said, gloomily.

They were in the Old Vienna, off the Strand, a wine bar that Zoe liked because the food often tasted slightly burnt, which gave her confidence that it didn't come from an imagined central cooking complex in Swindon pre-packaged for microwaving.

'It's only a tooth, you said.'

'I know.'

'Forty-eight hours, you said.'

'I know.'

'I'll be with you every evening, you said.'

'I know.'

'So where were you last night?'

'Yesterday was a bastard. I had to go to Suffolk. When I got back there was a siege in a council flat in Westminster, a man holding a young girl. That didn't end till three in the morning and it was too late to phone you. I was so bloody tired I went home to bed.'

'Home?' she said. 'What's that? Oh, yes, I remember. It's our flat in Pimlico.'

'Did you have a dull evening?'

Dull, she thought, was not a word she would have chosen. Advertising copywriters had to be precise in their use of words. Boring, tedious, wearing, frustrating . . . those were some. Then there were others such as rage, fury, violence, frenzy, hysteria, that also sprang to mind.

She had had her dinner with Manfred.

'Do you know what is *backhendl*?' he asked when she came in.

She had decided not to be bullied by Manfred. 'Is that Willibald Backhendl who wrote the famous concerto for glass harmonica and kettle drum?'

He stared at her unhappily. This is what you got from a mother who lived in a commune and ate nuts. What had he done that God should have visited this woman on his only son?

'*Backhendl* is fried chicken in the style of Vienna.'

'We're having steak and chips,' she said. 'How do you like yours?'

After supper she asked him if he was going to his chess club. He shook his head. She picked up the paper and decided to endure Manfred until Leo got back.

'Leo tells me you like music.'

'That's right.'

'What?'

For a long moment her mind went completely blank. She could not think of a single composer or a single piece of music.

Manfred said, 'Johann Bach's Greatest Hits?'

Stung, she said, 'Not at all. I like a lot of things. I studied the piano at school.'

This did not impress Manfred, the music teacher. 'You want to listen to something?'

She thought he meant a tape, instead he led her to the music-room and sat down at the Bosendorfer. There was only the straight-backed chair he used for his lessons and she sat down on that.

'You know Sorabji?' He played a few bars that sounded vaguely like a sitar transcribed for keyboard. 'Opus Clavicembalisticum. Four and a half hours. No repeats. The longest keyboard piece in the world (*vurld*).'

'Why would—?'

Manfred played a few bars of another piece. 'Satie. Vexations. You can play it for ever, but it is all repeats.'

'Would you like some coffee?'

He ignored her. 'They want long pieces? I can give them long pieces.' He began to play.

It sounded to Zoe as though he was playing a series of studies by Czerny. He played first with one hand, then the other, then both together. He did 'shakes' and arpeggios. She began to feel he was making it up as he went along to pay her back for the Vienna chicken.

He played for an hour. Zoe's bottom became numb. She fought sleep, anger, and despair. She felt that at any moment she would fall off the chair and foam at the mouth.

Where was Leo?

Manfred played on. He played roulades, he played a series of octaves in contrary motion, he played allegro vivace, he played allegro con fuoco, he played lento, he played—

Miraculously, the phone rang. She leapt from the chair and ran to the next room.

'Who is it?' Manfred said.

'A Mrs Benjamin. She says Morris is sick and can't come for his lesson tomorrow.'

'Morris is always sick. You want to listen some more?'

'It was wonderful, really wonderful. But I must go to bed.'

'I will have a cup of tea.'

'I'll make you one.'

'Don't forget to warm the pot.'

In the Old Vienna, Leo nodded unhappily. 'I know that piece. The Antaeus Variations. He's been working on it for years.'

'Leo, why doesn't he write small pieces? I mean everything's so big. The Falklands Symphony. Two orchestras and God knows how many choirs. Then that opera based on the Diet of Worms. Can't you explain to him about miniatures? Can't you get him to write the smallest not the biggest? You know, symphonies for six instruments. Or the shortest keyboard pieces ever written.'

'I wish we could. The variations drive my mother mad. The whole family for that matter. He's got no one to play them to any more.'

'Except me.'

'Except you. What can I say?'

'You can say Zoe, darling, I'm going to fetch my mother and take her back to her husband. Then I'm going to take you out for a nice dinner. Then I'm going to take you home. Home! And I'm going to take you to your own bed and—'

'For God's sake keep your voice down.'

' . . . and let you sleep. What did you think I was going to say?'

'You want another drink?'

'You've got a dirty mind, Leo. I've always thought so. Yes, please. Oh, and who made the magic go out of our marriage? You or me? I've been saving that.'

'Stop quoting Thurber at me.'

When he came back with the drinks she said, 'What's happened about the Macrae thing?'

'That's why I went to Suffolk.'

He told her about his talk with Waddell.

She frowned, uncomprehending. 'But what's it got to do with Macrae?'

'It's obvious, isn't it?'

'No, Leopold, it isn't. He tells you he thinks Artie Gorman might have used Stoker to warn off this man who isn't Thrush or Budgie or whatever, and the warning – in the vernacular – goes "a bit over the top". So what's that— Oh, I see! If you can get something on Stoker you can make him back off from Macrae.'

'Something like that.'

'It sounds feasible.'

'The morality doesn't bother you?'

'No, I don't think so. Listen, women are supposed to be pragmatic. Sexy and attractive, but also pragmatic. This Stoker is a real horror. So what do you do with horrors? You eliminate them as best you can. End of story.'

'That simple?'

'Precisely.'

'Well, I don't like it. I don't—'

'Oh, for God's sake, Leo, if it was the other way round Macrae wouldn't hesitate. It's called loyalty.'

He looked at her uneasily. 'I suppose so. Anyway I've asked for a print-out on the life and times of Honest Arthur Gorman. That may give me a line.'

'OK, so we've solved that one. You can always say to yourself now: "Zoe made me do it." Why can't we solve our own affairs as simply?'

'They're really lovely,' Linda Macrae said, looking at the rich wall hangings in Irene's sitting-room.

'They come from a place near Cordoba. I went with . . . a

friend. You can see the Moorish patterns. There's still a lot of Moorish influence in that part of Andalucia. What can I get you?'

'Gin and tonic?'

Irene got the drinks and they sat opposite each other on low divans covered in Spanish throw-rugs. The room glowed in reds and yellows.

'God, what a day!' Irene said. 'Are your parents still alive?'

'No.'

'You're lucky. No, no, I shouldn't say that. What I mean is that there are some old people who would be better off—' She stopped. 'I'm getting tangled up. It's just that I've spent the day with my . . . with my friend and her elderly mother. We took her out to lunch.'

She sketched in briefly what had happened to her 'friend's' mother.

Linda laughed. 'I shouldn't, of course, but . . . the bar stool. Did she really? And the waiter . . . ?'

There was a pause then Linda said, 'Is there anything you need to know about the house? I may be going away and there won't be anyone to ask.'

'I think I'm OK. Somewhere hot and sunny?'

'I hope so, but I doubt it. Inverness.'

'Don't bet on it.'

Irene waited but Linda did not expand. In fact Linda had nothing to expand with. No arrangements had been made – not positively anyway. David Leitman was supposed to phone her at ten and if he repeated his invitation to come up to Scotland she was going to accept. And if he didn't she was going to work the conversation round to it – and *then* accept. Was it the arrival of Irene that had caused her to rethink her arguments? It had certainly concentrated her mind.

'Is that someone at the front door?' Irene said.

The front door of the house was above them.

'Maybe someone for you or Mr Leitman.'

'We can't hear either bell from here.' Linda got to her feet. There was the banging of the door knocker.

'I'd better go and see,' Linda said.

Linda went up the basement stairs. Irene stood in her hall where she could watch. The light was on in the porch and even before Linda reached the steps that led to the front door she recognized the figure of the man standing there. He bent down, rattled the letter box flap, and peered through.

'You won't see anything through that, George.'

Macrae straightened up quickly. The blood flowed suddenly from his head and he felt giddy. He staggered slightly and steadied himself on the door frame.

'I couldn't get an answer,' he said.

She had noticed the slight unsteadiness, now she registered the thickness of his voice. She had heard it many times in the past.

'What is it?' she said.

She found these visits disturbing. For many years after their marriage foundered she had not seen George. He had gone off, married Mandy, had children by her, was divorced by her. Occasionally she had seen him on TV when he was in charge of a major investigation.

But recently their daughter Susan, now grown up, had needed money for a once-in-a-lifetime trip to Indonesia and Australia and the amount was too steep for Linda to bear on her own. She had reluctantly gone to George for three thousand pounds. And this, against her will, had reopened doors she thought were permanently closed. George had begun to make little visits.

'I wanted to see you,' Macrae said.

'What for?'

'Are you going to ask me in?' As he said it he flinched, for he had used the phrase to Mandy.

'No, George, I'm not.'

'Whatsa . . . where the hell did you spring from anyway?'

'A new tenant has moved into the garden flat. I was having a drink with her. What is it, George? Is it important?'

'It's a friendly visit, that's all.'

'Look, you've got to stop this. I can't have you coming round here and—'

'Why ever not? There's nothing to say a man and his ex shouldn't be friends.'

'Yes, there is. In this case the ex says so. If you want to rewrite domestic history then go and rewrite it with Mandy.'

The porch light was above him and she could see his heavy face change. She knew what he was like when he was angry. She had hurt his pride – and George had more than most – and she was sorry, but enough was enough.

'To hell with you, then!'

He went off down the steps and along the street and she could hear the door of his car slam.

She went back to Irene's. 'Sorry about that.' There were question marks in Irene's eyes and Linda thought of saying it was someone selling double-glazing, but what was the point?

'Detective Superintendent George Macrae, my ex.'

'You should have brought him down. He could have had a drink.'

'He couldn't stay.'

Irene waited but Linda did not expand further.

Macrae drove back to Battersea. He felt humiliated and angry. What made it worse was that the anger was directed at himself. What a bloody fool he'd made of himself! He'd gone with his tail between his legs to see if she could lend him a couple of thousand and he'd had to brace himself with a few drinks first. And of course that was the worst possible way to do it. He'd have to go round and apologize sometime. Thank God he hadn't mentioned the money.

He went into his house. It was cold and dark and unwelcoming. He gave himself a large Scotch and drank half in a gulp. The anger did not lessen, instead it increased to a cold rage, but its focus changed.

Stoker.

This was all happening because of Stoker.

Macrae sat down, nursing the whisky, and brooded. Right at the start he had rejected the elimination of Stoker but that was before things had reached this stage. He recapped. Already the rumour was out that a senior copper was bent. Soon, if he didn't comply, a name would be dropped. He couldn't frighten Stoker off. It seemed that he couldn't raise any money.

Well, if those were the parameters and if the only way to solve the problem was the removal of Stoker then removed he would have to be.

There were men Macrae had served with in the Force, hard men, who now worked in private security firms, who would not

109

think twice about removing Stoker. But they'd want plenty of bread and he hadn't got it. However, there was one man who might do. He had left the police under a cloud. There had been talk of him beating a suspect half to death in the cells at Savile Row. Macrae had saved his arse so he owed him. Rampton. DI Billy Rampton. Where the hell had he lived? South of the river somewhere. Peckham or Catford.

He gave himself another whisky and picked up the London phone book to check his address. Even as he did so he said out loud: 'Stop it!'

This was the whisky talking and he knew it. There was no way he would be a party to the killing of Stoker. Not that he had any moral feelings one way or the other about the loss of Stoker to society. No, it was too bloody complicated and too dangerous.

But thinking of Billy Rampton turned his thoughts in another direction. Billy had been working in private security. The word was that Billy was making his pile. It was time to call in his debt.

It was four o'clock in the morning and Gladys Twyford was awake. She lay in her bed staring at the ceiling. The heavy rock beat from the apartment next door expanded and contracted in her brain like a purple light.

'I can't stand it,' she told herself. 'I'm going mad.'

She had barricaded herself in as usual about four o'clock in the afternoon. She had looked at a newspaper and a magazine. Then, about six, she had put out the light and dozed for a few hours.

The music had woken her and she had been lying awake ever since. If things followed their usual pattern the noise would stop about five. Then she would get a couple more hours' sleep.

It was this lying awake that drove her to the edge of sanity. If she had been able to read she would have got through the night more easily – that's how she thought of it, 'getting through the night'. But she was afraid that putting on the lights might draw attention to her. The darkness made her feel invisible. It was like that eye contact that Eddie had warned her about. Lights were like eyes and might offend them.

On her last visit to the shops she had bought a box of wax earplugs. They helped. It was as though the music was suddenly shifted about a hundred yards further away from her. But then she had thought: what if they come into the flat? What if they move the kitchen table or break a window?

'What if I can't hear them?' she had said to bulldog.

She needed all her senses: hearing, sight, and smell.

'What if they set the place on fire? What do we do then?'

She was not a cruel person, but she hoped that the woman in hospital, the one who was down for a flat in Briar House, would just stay there.

'Hospital is nice,' she said to bulldog. 'She'll be looked after.'

And then a terrible thought entered her mind: What if the lady remained in hospital but the flat went to someone else; someone who could pay the administration costs?

That was the key. The money. Somehow she had to find the administration costs.

14

Marshall & Masters, Estate Agents, Surveyors & Valuers, Est. 1953, was located off Clapham High Street. Irene paused at the window. She could see into the single-room office. Gerald was not visible but an elderly man in a dark striped suit and blue striped shirt was sitting at a desk in one corner.

'Good morning, Madame.' He inflected the last word in the French manner as Irene entered, and rose to his feet.

He was tall and still had all his own hair. It was silvery grey and swept back in waves. He touched it as he spoke as though subconsciously directing her attention to it.

'Is Gerald Masters in?' Irene said.

'I'm afraid he's out with a client. I'm Mr Marshall, the senior partner. Is there anything I can do?'

He wore a gold chain across his stomach and a large gold signet ring on his left hand. His tie was club or school. There was a dandified air about him and a slight smell of lemon-scented verbena. He looked like something out of a 1930s clothing catalogue. His face reminded her of a tortoise, even to the wrinkled skin at his neck.

'I'm Irene Isard. I've rented the garden flat at 15 Alma Road and he asked me to call in to sign the dilapidations.'

With a flourish, Marshall offered her a chair and went to the other desk and rummaged among a mound of papers.

'It's quite easy to file things,' he said, irritably. 'There are filing cabinets. But this is always the first place I look.'

Gerald had told her he was a doddering old man whose presence in the office was just about tolerated. His attitude belied this, so did his description of himself.

He pulled a piece of paper from the pile. 'That's where the young—' He stopped suddenly.

'That's right. That's where the young woman lived who killed herself.'

'Oh, so you knew.'

'Yes, I knew.'

He waited for her to continue but she remained silent.

'Can I sign it now? I mean I don't have to wait for Gerald, do I?'

He looked at her questioningly. 'Do you know Gerald? I mean outside of the agency?'

'I should have called him Mr Masters, I suppose.'

'Mister Masters. Bit of a mouthful. I call him Gerry, or the boy racer.'

'The Porsche?'

'Exactly.'

There was something sharp and malicious about the way he said it, and Irene was surprised then intrigued.

As she pulled the paper towards her Marshall, with a second flourish, handed her an expensive fountain pen. There was something familiar about it, as though she had seen it before somewhere.

She was conscious of him watching her as she signed.

'Do you know Clapham?' he asked.

'I've never lived south of the river before.'

'Then you won't know the Zanzibar.'

She shook her head.

'Allow me to introduce you.'

'Now?'

'It is practically next door.' He looked at his watch. 'And the sun's over the yardarm.'

'No, thanks, it's a bit early for me.'

'You have a rendezvous?'

He made it sound like something out of a *film noir*.

'No. Not really.'

'You'd be doing me a favour. I don't often have company.'

She did not want a drink but there was something about the old man that both attracted and repelled her. She was confused.

113

It was as though she had met him somewhere before. But the reason she went was that he had somehow made her responsible for his happiness and it would have been churlish to refuse. She wasn't quite sure how he had managed that.

The Zanzibar was a 'club' of the kind she thought had gone out in the sixties. It was in a basement and was in the early stages of opening for the day. There was a smell of strong soap and stale smoke. The word 'tacky' came to mind but again it brought to her a puzzling sense of *déjà vu*.

It was dark in the way that American bars are dark. And the darkness hid the tackiness of the bamboo furniture and the fake potted palms. The walls were covered by travel posters of Zanzibar, Tanzania, and Kenya. Elephants and lions glowered down at her.

'Large G and T for me,' Marshall said to the black bartender who was wearing a red fez on his head. 'What about you, dear lady? May I call you Irene? My name, by the way, is Harold.'

'A small sherry.'

'A small sherry for my guest, Mustapha.'

She thought that everything Marshall did had the words 'olde worlde charm' attached to it.

'Cheers.'

'Cheers. Did you know the previous tenant?'

'Saw her once or twice. Gerald brought her by. Pale little thing. Gerald knows everyone. Or says he does.'

Again there was the slight undercurrent of malice.

'I wonder why he takes that great dog around with him?' she said, attuning herself to his mood.

'Macho man.' He pronounced it 'macko'. 'Anyway, let's not talk about Gerald. Another?'

She saw that he had already finished his drink while she had hardly sipped hers.

'No? A duplicate, Mustapha, please.'

'It's strange being in a place where the previous tenant was so unhappy.'

'Unhappy?'

'Well, she must have been. She killed herself.'

'Let us not be gloomy. She is dead beyond recall.'

'You're right. Let's not.' She took another sip. The sherry was dreadful, it tasted as though it had been manufactured out of chemicals. 'Gerald was saying that his mother worked with you.'

'*For* me. She was my typist.'

'Oh, I thought she was a partner.'

'Good God! Mavis? Not on your life.' He laughed at the absurdity of it. 'Damn good sergeant-major, but never an officer – if you get what I mean?'

'I think so.' And then abruptly she said, 'Were you in the army?'

He touched his tie. 'Royal Hants Fusiliers. Why?'

'I just wondered. You have a military bearing.'

He touched his silvery grey hair, then said, 'Don't be fooled by Gerald. He sounds public school but isn't. Mavis did her best for him. She was as tough as old boots.'

'So you took him in?'

'Well, I saw some promise there. Felt a bit sorry for him too after she'd worked on him. There's just so much you can knock into someone. I mean you've got to show a bit of kindness, damn it all.'

He fitted a cigarette into a black holder.

Click.

Into the frame of memory came Aldershot and Bordon and a dozen other bleak army camps. The rows of married quarters. The clubs in Cyprus and Malaya that in retrospect reminded her of the Zanzibar. Her father, Major Victor Isard. Later, in civvie street, the Major.

This was the kind of place he would have used. There were dozens of them twenty years ago: bamboo, palm trees, Formica. And had he lived he might have looked and dressed like Harold Marshall: gents' natty suitings, cigarette holder, membership of the Zanzibar. Boozing here all day with men who were also anachronisms, then staggering off home to beat the daylights out of his wife – and his daughter if he could catch her.

'I have to be going,' she said.

'Look here, Irene . . . ' He placed his hand over hers. 'What about a spot of lunch? Not here. There's a Thai place across the road. Not at all bad.'

115

'Some other time,' she said and twisted her hand away.

'Right . . . absolutely . . . some other time.'

Leo Silver was out of his depth. He needed someone to talk to, needed someone to guide him. Above all he needed Macrae, yet he was the one person he couldn't go to. The thought of going to Scales had not even entered his mind.

He was not given to self-doubt. But today he was feeling somewhat sorry for himself and he knew why: it was isolation, plus being burdened with something he considered grossly unfair. He was angry with Scales. He was angry with Macrae. He was angry with circumstances.

He phoned Zoe.

'Lunch?' she said. 'Yummy. Where?'

'I'll meet you in Hyde Park at the Albert Memorial.'

'I know a marvellous Italian place just off Knightsbridge. What did you do, stick up a bank?'

She was waiting for him dressed in a black coat and white cashmere scarf and black knee-length boots. He felt like rushing her across to the nearest hotel and giving her something to remember him by.

She looked into the brown paper bag he was carrying which contained two tuna-salad sandwiches and two coffees.

'What an original idea,' she said, as they sat on the steps of the Albert Memorial. 'A picnic in midwinter.'

But Leo was too preoccupied to respond. 'I found out something about Artie Gorman that could make a difference,' he said.

'To Macrae?'

'If I can play things right.'

'That's why the picnic? Boy sleuth needs help?'

'It's just that I've got no one else to talk to about it.'

'Thank you, Leo, that's nicely put.'

He took a foolscap envelope from his coat pocket and drew out two sheets of paper. 'The first is from Criminal Records at the Yard. Honest Arthur had quite a bit of form in his early career: there's receiving stolen property . . . fraud . . . a little mild extortion . . . a year, two years, some suspended. Then later he becomes respectable. And there's no link with a murder on Primrose Hill – or anywhere else for that matter.'

'So that lets out Stoker.'

'Not necessarily. Just because there's no reference doesn't mean Arthur didn't get him to do it.'

'No, what I meant was it means you haven't got anything to frighten Stoker with. You can't go to him and say, "Look here, Stoker, old bean, you'd better not, etc. . . . etc. . . ." '

'You're sending it up.'

'Only because you're so grim-faced about it. Anyway, I know you too well. You didn't invite me out for this delicious lunch – by the way it is fish isn't it, and not some sort of soya thing? OK, OK – well, you didn't invite me here just to say you had nothing.'

'No.'

'Good. Because I'm freezing.'

'Her name is Slattery.'

'Whose name?'

'Molly Gorman née Slattery. Says so in Artie's file. With the date of the marriage, etc., so I thought, you know, that I'd run a check on her.'

'And?'

'Nothing in Criminal Records. Clean as a whistle. But . . . ' He lingered on the word.

'I knew there was a but. Come on, Leo.'

'So I asked at the General Registry.'

'Never heard of it.'

'No reason why you should. It's also at the Yard. It keeps a record of any correspondence or any contact the general public has with the police. There's nothing there about Artie Gorman—'

'Molly Gorman née Slattery?'

'Right.' He looked around at the surrounding area at the base of the memorial as though expecting to be overheard and then, in a lowered voice, said, 'She was an informer.'

'A police informer?' The levity had vanished.

They stared at each other in silence as she digested this piece of information.

'This was long ago, before she married Artie. She was only a kid really but she was mixed up with people who were mixed up with the Krays.'

'Didn't they make a movie about the Krays?'

'A kind of British *Godfather*. You wouldn't go to it. The point is the Krays are like royalty to the villains in the East End. Even though they've been inside for years the people there still revere them. What d'you think Stoker would do if he found out Molly had been an informer? I mean to people like Stoker you can't get any lower.'

'*Cherchez la femme*,' she said.

'Right.'

All Gladys wanted was to get back to her flat.

When she was in it and the noise from next door was unbearable, she would have given anything to be somewhere else.

But not now.

Now it was home. Sanctuary.

She had been humiliated. She was frightened. Ahead lay no man's land. Behind was Mr Geach.

He hadn't recognized her. That had been the first thing. Simply hadn't known who she was or what she was talking about. He was eating – a pork pie, she thought – and he said, 'Didn't you see the notice? Can't you read?'

He had spoken with his mouth full and for a moment she had not understood him. He got up from his desk and held the door so that she could see the notice. It said: 'Closed for Lunch 1–2 p.m.'

'I'm sorry,' she said.

'You people are *always* sorry.'

She adjusted her scarf and settled her handbag under her arm but made no move to go.

The tufts of hair on Mr Geach's head seemed, like transplanted grass, to be dying.

'I'm having my lunch. Come back later.'

It had taken courage for Gladys to come at all and she could never do it twice in one day, specially when the afternoon began to draw to a close – which wasn't much later than half-past three these days.

'I come about the money,' she said.

'What money?'

'The administration costs.'

He peered at her, his jaw working all the while.

'You been before?'

'Just the other day. It's Mrs Twyford. Rosemary.'

She explained their previous meeting.

'Oh, yeah, didn't recognize you in the scarf.'

'Five hundred pounds, you said.'

He gave her a calculating look. 'In cash.'

'In cash.'

'And then there's the Stamp Duty.'

'The Stamp Duty? What's that?'

'You got to have Stamp Duty. It's the law. Makes everything official.'

'How much is that?'

'That's another fifty.'

'So it's five hundred and fifty?'

'That's it.'

She paused. He took a bite of raised pastry.

'I been thinking,' she said. 'I've only got my pension and Mr Twyford's. I could pay you – I worked it out – I could pay you five pounds a month for the administration costs – and the Stamp Duty.'

He looked at her in disbelief. 'On the never-never? You must be joking! You want to move from Rosemary to Briar and you want to pay five pounds a month? There're old folk who'd give their left arms for a flat in Briar.'

'It's all I can afford.'

'Don't waste my time. Don't come round here with your five-pounds-a-month talk. Why that's . . . For Christ's sake it'd take nearly ten years!' He lost his temper. 'Go on, get out!'

She found herself outside his office. She was trembling from a mixture of humiliation and anxiety. It had seemed so reasonable. She'd worked it out in the depths of the night. And he'd lost his temper.

She had to get home. She could make herself a cup of tea and go over things. Think things out, as Eddie used to say.

There *had* to be a way.

Start, she said. Put one foot ahead of the other. She was talking to bulldog even though he wasn't there.

Soon she would be at Rosemary.

119

And don't look up, no matter who said what. No eye contact.

She began her journey.

The fog was being swept along by a brisk and freezing wind. And it swept Gladys Twyford along with it. She was propelled along the concrete paths, past the car wrecks and the broken playground.

But she did not notice them. All she saw, as the wind pressed into her back, were the cracks in the paths through which weeds were struggling.

Then she saw a foot in a boot, then another and another. Army boots.

Before she could stop herself, she glanced up. They were standing in a semicircle, five of them, looking at her.

Oh God, she thought. Them.

Quickly she lowered her eyes and stepped on to the muddy grass.

They stepped off too.

Terror gripped her.

One of them said, 'She's the old bitch from Rosemary. The one with the husband who was a copper.'

'But he ain't no more,' said a second.

'Pisshead,' said a third.

They were a blur to her. She could not recognize individuals. God knew how old they were: fourteen? fifteen? They all looked alike to her.

'Where you going, you old cow?'

'That's not nice. Not an old cow. You got to respect old age. Call her missus.'

'Where you going, missus, you old cow? That OK?'

'Croucher. Why you crouching, Croucher?'

'Missus Croucher.'

Hilarious!

'Gi' us your bag, you old crouching bag.'

Fantastic!

They pulled her bag from under her arm.

They're going to rape me, she thought. They're going to take me into one of the deserted hallways and all of them are going to do it. Gang rape. The phrase had lain dormant in her mind. Now it was out – like a tiger.

120

They emptied the bag on the ground: pension-book, keys, comb, pills, letters, Eddie's long-service medal. They kicked them.

'Any money?'

'Couple of quid.'

One reached forward, grabbed the headscarf, and pulled it down over her eyes.

They turned her round and round.

Brilliant!

She reached out her hands to stop the spinning world and the earth came up into her face. She tasted mud.

By the time she had managed to collect her senses and regain her sight, they had gone: a line of young boys disappearing into the mist.

She found she was making a continuous dirge-like sound. There were no tears, just this anguished noise.

She came up on her knees and began to collect her things, her bits and pieces that had been trampled into the mud.

15

Macrae parked the Rover at the end of the short street and eased his big body into a more comfortable position. He would have liked to change the angle of the seat so he could lie back but, like several other knobs and levers in the car, the knob that controlled the seat no longer worked.

Billy Rampton wasn't home. He'd called a short while before. He didn't just want to walk in on him cold. He'd have to now.

His stomach was full of wind and there was a sour taste in his mouth. Sausages and two pints of beer for lunch hadn't been the best idea but he knew that no matter what he'd eaten the result would have been the same. Ever since he'd had the barney with Stoker he'd been feeling more and more tense. He'd been smoking and drinking more than usual with the result that his stomach had gone bad on him.

He was aware that the next hour or so was going to be bloody awful. Going to someone like Billy for money was a humiliation Macrae could hardly bear, but it would have been ten times worse going to a fellow officer.

But there was simply no other way.

He'd even considered going back to Molly, begging her for old times' sake. But when he recalled her face after the things he'd said about Stoker he knew there was nothing she would do. She might even tell Stoker – probably would – and he could not stand the thought of that.

A car pulled up outside number forty-nine. It was dusk and Macrae could only make out a shadowy figure. But the figure unlocked the door and went in. Billy Rampton had come home.

Macrae waited another few minutes, then he strolled along the street and rang the bell.

It was a small terraced house with a bow window at the front. In the old days the room would have been called the front parlour. They'd had a front parlour when Macrae was a kid. Only used on Sundays or when there were visitors. He remembered the three-piece suite. It had come from one of the cheap furniture shops in the Lothian Road in Edinburgh: fake leopard-skin with black leather inserts.

He rang again.

He thought he saw a curtain twitch. Billy was playing things very close to the chest.

'Billy!' Macrae called through the letter flap. 'It's George Macrae.'

He heard a step, then the rattle of locks, then the drawing of serious security bolts. The door opened on a chain. The passage was dark.

'George?'

'Yes. It's me, Billy.'

The chain came off. 'Come in, George.'

Macrae entered the dark, chilly hallway and the door was quickly locked and bolted again. He found his hand being pumped.

'George! Christ, it's good to see you. It's been a long time.'

'Aye. A long time.'

He followed Rampton into the sitting-room/parlour. Rampton made sure the curtains were tightly drawn then he put the lights on. 'Can't be too careful,' he said.

Macrae glanced around. The room was anonymous, just greys and fawns with artificial leather furniture and a gas-log fire. He hadn't seen Billy for several years. He would not have recognized him. At Savile Row police station he'd been the man you didn't want to trifle with, not if you were a villain, not if you were another copper: big, black-haired, black-eyed.

'You heard then, George. It's bloody good of you to come round. Haven't seen any of the old firm. Not one. Here let me get you a drink. Scotch was always your tipple wasn't it?' He began to search in cupboards. As far as Macrae could see they were filled with empty cider flagons.

Was this Billy Rampton? *The* Billy Rampton?

The man on his knees searching through cupboards of empties

123

was hardly even the ghost of Billy Rampton. He had lost weight. His clothes hung awkwardly on his bony frame. There was a long angry scar on the side of his head and Macrae could see little puncture marks where stitches had been removed.

'Thought I had some, George . . . What about cider?'

'Don't worry.'

'No, no, we must.'

He found a half-full flagon. The cider was flat and smelled horrible but George raised his glass. 'Here's to you, Billy.'

'God, it's good to see you, George. I knew . . . I bloody knew that if anyone came it would be big George Macrae. When did you hear what happened to me?'

Macrae played safe. 'Only a couple of days ago.'

'Jesus, news used to travel quicker than that. Anyway, no matter . . . No fucking matter . . . Sit, George. Sit. Listen, have a cigar. You used to smoke those thin cigars didn't you?'

'Aye. Still do.'

'See? Memory still bloody good. I used to have some. I'll have a look.'

'No, no, Billy. I've got plenty.'

'You want a cigarette?'

'Never use them.'

'Bloody wise.'

Billy lit a cigarette and inhaled deeply.

'You look great, George. Great.'

'You too, Billy. How's Val?'

'Val? Didn't you hear? She left me for a bloody rep selling greetings cards. A bloody salesman in a white Ford Sierra!'

'I'm sorry to hear that, Billy.'

'We're two of a kind, George. Two of a kind.'

Macrae frowned, he wasn't ready for that. Instead he said, 'I came as soon as I heard.'

'That's what I said to myself in hospital. I said they don't *know*. They'd come if they knew.'

'Tell me about it, Billy.'

Rampton took another long pull on his cigarette. Macrae noticed that his fingers were badly stained by smoke.

'You ever come across a villain called Joe Fentiman?'

124

'Can't recall the name.'

'You will. He's one of the new lot south of the River. The days of the old East End gangs are over now, George. The party's moved south. Bloody Pakistanis and Turks and Christ knows what are running things down that way now. Anyway, this Fentiman sod has got a liquor warehouse down Tooting way. And he specializes in cases of this and that, selling them off at half the price – wines and gin and Bacardi and stuff like that.

'I was working for a liquor company called Three Ways. You ever heard of them? No? Well, no reason why you should. Importers, wholesalers, etc., etc. . . And they're always losing stuff. A few cases here, fifty cases there. You know the score. Truck pulls into a transport café, driver goes in for tea and a bacon sarny. And when he drives off he's a few cases light. Maybe ten, maybe twenty or thirty. And he knows because he's been slipped a few quid and told where to park the lorry.'

'I know the score.'

'Course you do, George. So, anyway, my lot say to me, Billy, you're the bloody security man, this has got to stop. Well, didn't take long to find out who was doing the thieving.'

'Joe Fentiman.'

'Yeah. Fentiman and his lads. Anyway, they heard I was on to them so Fentiman comes to see me. Right here in this house. And offers me five hundred quid to look the other way.

'I said to him, you must be joking, my son, you're pulling in thousands and thousands – I mean Three Ways is losing about a hundred grand a year and that's only one company. So he says take it or leave it.

'So I said he could stuff it. I said make me a decent offer or get lost. Know what I mean?'

He lit another cigarette.

'He didn't like that. He was big but not too big – and you know me George. Ready for anything.

'So he says OK . . . OK . . . let's talk some more. Let me go and see my people. We didn't know you was serious. So I said OK, you go and talk to your people. And I'm just closing the door when three of his lads – I mean I thought I'd been bloody careful – but anyway these three lads pushed the door in and Fentiman comes back, that makes four, and they laid into me. Iron bars. Chains. You name it.'

His voice had dropped. 'That's when I copped this.' He pointed to the recently healed wound on his head. 'And this.' He pulled up his shirt and Macrae saw three or four livid scars on his chest and back. 'Then they wrecked the place. This is all new secondhand. I tell you, George, I nearly snuffed it.'

'Hard men.'

'Yeah, very hard. Nearly a month in hospital. Intensive care. Tubes everywhere. Have some more.' He held up the cider flagon.

'No thanks. I've got a bad gut.'

He poured the remainder into his glass. 'Tastes like piss,' he said. 'Still, better than nothing.'

'But you're OK now, Billy?'

'OK? Look at that.' He held out his hand. 'Trembles like a fucking leaf. Can't do a thing to stop it. They fixed me, George. I'm not ashamed to say it. And in more ways than one. When I got out of hospital the firm made me redundant.'

'I'm sorry to hear that.'

'Said it was the recession, the bastards, but they took on someone else a few weeks later. Didn't even give me a decent handshake. Just what they were obliged to pay by law.'

He rose and went to the window, pulled the curtains back an inch and peered into the street. 'Sometimes I think they'll . . . They won't be back, will they? I mean there's no reason now.'

'They won't come back, Billy. As you say, there's no reason.' Macrae rose. 'I'm on duty in half an hour. Just thought I'd drop in and see how you were.'

'That's bloody good of you, George. Really good. You were always the best.'

They went out into the hallway. 'Listen George. I hate doing this, specially to someone like you. But you couldn't lend me a couple of hundred could you? I'll pay you back once I get a job. You know you can trust me. You have my word on that.'

126

Macrae felt burning gas come up into his throat. 'Course I can trust you, Billy. But, laddie, you've got to believe me when I say I couldn't even lend you a tenner. Not even a fiver.'

There was something in the way he said it that was entirely convincing. 'Women?' Rampton said.

'Well, not so much women as children.'

'That's one small mercy. Val and I never had any.'

At the door Rampton said, 'Excuse me for asking, George.'

'Don't be bloody silly.'

They shook hands.

'They were great days, George. I mean at Savile Row. Great days. The villains knew who was boss, didn't they?'

'Aye, Billy, they certainly knew that. By the way, Billy, did you ever come across a villain called Stoker? Assaulted a PC in Hackney some years back?'

Rampton thought for a moment and then slowly shook his head. 'Don't think so. Why?'

'Just wondered. Look after yourself.'

'Yeah. You too, George.'

Macrae heard the door close behind him, then the clashing of the locks and bars and bolts and chains.

He put his hands in his pockets, hunched forward against the wind, and walked down the street to his car.

The letter came in the afternoon mail and was addressed to Miss Grace Davies. Irene looked at it for a long moment then opened it. At first, because it took her by surprise, it confused her. It also tore at her heart that anyone should still think Grace was alive.

She looked again at the heading on the single sheet of notepaper: Kingswood Publishers. The address was in Covent Garden. The letter read:

Dear Miss Davies,

You said you would let me know what to do with the typescript of IN THE FORESTS OF THE NIGHT. I don't want to send it by post in case you've moved as you said you might

127

and in case you don't have a copy. Could you let me know, please?

I'm sorry things didn't work out. As I said at the time, I thought there was a good idea for a commercial novel here but that you were too close to it.

Yours sincerely,
Juliette Simmonds
Senior Editor

Irene frowned and read it through again. Typescript? Novel? Grace must have been writing all this time. She stared out at the unkempt back garden as dusk settled on London.

Grace. A novelist!

She must talk to Miss Juliette Simmonds. And she must get back the typescript.

She reached forward to dial the number on the notepaper, when the phone rang. She recoiled, as though it was alive.

'This is Dr Malhotra,' the voice said. 'At Linwood House. Your mother is one of my patients.'

Irene felt a cold hand grip her bowels. It was a feeling she had had many times over the years whenever those in charge of her mother got into sudden contact with her. It was never anything pleasant.

'Is she all right?' Irene asked, and part of her mind hoped for her mother's sake that she was not, that he was ringing to tell her she had slipped away from the battered shell of her body.

'She was the last time I saw her.'

'So why are you phoning me?'

'Well, I was wondering if she was with you. But it does not seem to be the case.'

'It certainly isn't the case!'

'You see she is not in the hospital. No one has seen her since breakfast time.'

'But it's nearly five. For goodness sake, don't you have checks?'

'Yes we do, and I am going to find out what went wrong. Do not worry about that.'

'But that's not the point.'

128

'Yes, yes, I know. We have started an inquiry. After breakfast there was Olde Tyme Dancing in the lounge by one of the Rotary Club groups. Your mother was seen by two of the nurses going towards the TV room.'

'She doesn't go to entertainments.'

'That is so, and therefore the nursing staff thought nothing of it.'

'Well, she isn't here and she isn't in the hospital. What do you propose?'

'We must alert the police.'

'No! Not yet. Give me a couple of hours. I think I know where she might be. She . . . well, I just think I might know.'

'But I'm afraid we cannot take the responsibility.'

'Responsibility! For God's sake, you let her out. That's not responsible, is it?'

There was a silence at the other end of the line. She wondered what Dr Malhotra was? Indian? Pakistani? Sri Lankan?

'I'm sorry,' she said. 'I shouldn't have gone off like that. Look, she's my mother. I've handled her in situations like this before. I'll have her back with you by seven or phone you. And then we can call the police. OK?'

'Sure. OK.'

Irene drove against the early rush-hour traffic, stopped once at a small suburban supermarket, and was coming into the Queenstown Road less than half an hour after taking the call. She parked, picked up her purchase, and walked back along the road. She turned left and left again and abruptly seemed to disappear from the urban scene.

She could hear, in the distance, the trains crossing the Thames on the Southern Railway. But apart from that she might have been in a foreign country. It was a place of broken fences, of ancient no trespassing notices, of almost illegible warnings about guard dogs, of mud and puddles, and torn paper streaming in the wind.

She picked her way through a hole in a fence and walked along a cinder track towards a coal wharf that had not been used for thirty years. She could see the black slick of the river under the lights on the opposite bank.

Once, large cranes had stood embedded in concrete platforms, but they had long since been removed, leaving huge holes like bomb craters. In one of these craters, around a small fire, sat a group of half a dozen people, men and women, as derelict as the site itself.

She heard the noise of someone hawking and spitting and then she saw her mother. She was sitting on the opposite side of the fire and her face was lit by the flames from burning driftwood.

Irene stopped, appalled. Although she could only have been there for some hours, Mrs Davies appeared, by her unkempt hair and generally ragged appearance, to have been part of the group for weeks or months.

It was like a replay. It had happened before. This was where she had been found and this was why Irene was not afraid to come alone. Twice before she had brought her mother out of this crater.

She had been afraid the first time. Then she had come with Grace's father. But when she saw the men with the cans of lager spiked with gin, when she saw what alcohol and sleeping rough had done to them physically, she knew she had little cause for fear.

This time, she had been clever.

As she went forward into the firelight the group turned hostile faces towards her.

'What d'you want?' a man said. He was dressed in an old topcoat fastened at the front with a large safety-pin. His grey hair had turned yellowish at the ends.

'This isn't television time. That's been and gone.' He coughed and spat. 'Come here with your bloody cameras!' His voice was educated.

'I'm not a television reporter,' Irene said.

'Every Christmas. Always the same. You come here and take a few pictures. Tell the world how bloody it's been to us. And then you piss off and we don't see you again for another year.'

Mrs Davies was looking at Irene over the flames but Irene knew she was not seeing anything. She was so drunk she could hardly keep her head up.

'I've brought you something,' Irene said to the group.

All she could see of them were their red faces in the firelight.

'We don't want your fucking charity,' a woman's voice said.

But Irene ignored her. She was carrying two six-packs of beer. Now she dropped them. There was a drunken scramble and she went round to the other side of the fire and put her hand under Mrs Davies' arm.

'Come on, Mother,' she said.

The old lady mumbled indistinctly but allowed herself to be hauled to her feet. She was so frail she weighed almost nothing.

'Goodnight,' Irene said as she led her mother along the cinder path. But the others were arguing fiercely and had no time to answer.

16

Leopold Silver — This is Your Home!

Zoe finished lettering the piece of white cardboard and pinned it on to the door of their maisonette so that it would be the first thing he saw when he came up the stairs from the street.

In other parts of the flat were signs like: 'This is Leo's teaspoon,' and 'This is Leo's chair.'

She had spent a happy half-hour thinking up things to amuse him when he came home.

Home!

She had come in and smelled the odours of stale garlic and unwashed socks and they had brought tears of joy to her eyes. Essence of Leo and Zoe.

It was such a lovely place to come home to. Warm yellows and oranges . . . sunny colours even in January. Then there were the dear chipped coffee mugs and the beloved dripping taps . . .

The point was they were *her* chipped mugs, and *her* dripping taps, and she didn't have to find an answer for questions like: *Why (vy) is that tap dripping?*

That was all finished. Lottie was back with Manfred in north-west London, and she was back with Leo – or would be when he got home – in south-west London, and although there weren't many miles between them, there were all sorts of barriers, like Hyde Park Corner and Marble Arch and traffic jams near Victoria . . . it didn't really matter which way you travelled, there were obstacles that made it nearly impossible for Manfred (who hated public transport) ever to get to Pimlico.

Free . . !

Wheee . . !

She lettered another card: 'Home is the Hunter, Home from the Hill!' and put it near the door. Later she would take it down and lay it on Leo's pillow. It might remind him of his conjugal duties – duties which had been sadly neglected in the emotionally restricting atmosphere of the senior Silvers' apartment.

Now . . .

First a long bath without a man's voice asking in broken English: 'Are you all right in there?'

Then, with the heating on full blast (Why do you not wear another jersey if you are cold?) she would make herself some cheese-and-tomato on toast (What are we having for dinner?) and curl up with a book or the TV and wait for Leo.

She felt as though she had been suddenly released from a women's prison. She had expected to be with Manfred for another night, then the phone – wonderful instrument – had rung and Lottie had been on the other end and the news had come that she was arriving home within the hour.

Zoe would always remember that moment. 'Where were you when the phone rang to say that Lottie Silver was coming home?'

'In the loo, m'lud.'

She giggled to herself.

'My wife is returning,' Manfred said. He made it sound as though she was struggling through some vast tundra instead of coming over from Kentish Town – correction, south Highgate.

He had then gone into the music-room and played something very fast and very loud. Zoe wasn't entirely sure what it was but it sounded like Liszt. She fled joyfully to the spare bedroom and began to pack.

'Poor *Liebchen*!' Lottie said, when she arrived. She gave Zoe a large hug. Then she sensed that this might have been a mistake, and said to her husband, 'Manfy!'

'You're back,' he said.

'Yes. I'm back.'

She embraced him while Sidney, their son-in-law, carried in her things.

'Hello, Dad,' he said. Zoe saw Manfred give him a withering look. She knew he hated Sidney calling him that.

'How's my daughter?' Manfred said, in lieu of a greeting.

133

'Fine, Dad.'

'Fine? I wish I was fine.'

'Now, Manfy . . . How have you been?' But before he could answer she turned to Zoe, 'How has he been? Bad?'

'No, of course not, Mrs Silver. We've got along just fine, haven't we, Mr Silver?'

Manfred did not reply to this, instead he said to Lottie, 'I haven't got any shirts.'

'Of course you have, I left a whole pile.'

'Not cotton ones.'

'For God's sake . . . No, no, we mustn't argue. Not now.' She began to tidy things.

Zoe had thought the room was tidy enough.

'How's Ruth's tooth, Mrs Silver?'

'How is the gap, more like it,' Manfred said. 'The tooth has gone.'

'I meant her jaw, really.'

'It's all right,' Sidney said. He was the husband, he was authoritative. 'A bit sore when she cleans but not so bad.'

'You mean she's brushing it already?' Zoe said, wincing.

'Not brushing,' Sidney said. 'The specialist says we've been doing it wrongly. He calls it wiggling. You get the brush up under the gum margins and you wiggle.'

'Wiggling!' Manfred said, appalled.

'I show you later,' Lottie said.

'It sounds pornographic,' Zoe said. 'But I suppose it's OK if you don't do it in the streets and frighten the horses.'

The moment she said it she knew it was a mistake. The Silvers – father, mother, and son-in-law – turned to look at her first in bewilderment, then irritation.

Now, in her own home she stripped off, walked naked into the bathroom, and turned on the water for her bath. She examined herself in the long mirror, put her hands on her hips, turned one way then the other, inspected her breasts, which Leo was wont to compare with lemons. She looked upon all this naked flesh with a certain satisfaction.

Then she said to her mirror image, 'Come home, Leo Silver. I'll give you wiggling.'

*

Macrae hated Sundays.

As a child he had lived in the village of Morile, a few miles north of Aviemore in the Central Highlands, whose religious focus was Free Presbyterian. And while his father was not religious – he was usually nursing a hangover on a Sunday – Macrae's grandparents were, and he was packed off to church with them.

His grandfather had been the blacksmith in the village and on Sundays his house was like the grave. He and Macrae's grandmother were strict. No work was done on Sundays, not even any cooking – the food was prepared the day before.

Macrae didn't mind not being allowed to work. But he greatly resented not being allowed to play once the long morning service was over. He couldn't fish, he couldn't go bird-nesting, he couldn't even read unless it was the Bible or the *Lives of the Saints*.

He lay in bed hating this January Sunday with particular venom. And, indeed, there was not a lot going for it. It was grey, it was cold, it was silent. And he was lonely. Frenchy was never there on a Sunday morning because Saturday night was her busiest time.

He read the papers, showered, made himself a cup of coffee, paced up and down, and smoked a thin cheroot. Then he stared at the blank TV screen and thought about switching it on, then thought that way lay madness. He put on his hat and coat and drove into Cannon Row.

He still had a few days of leave left to him but he couldn't stand it much longer. He was not a holiday person. The thought of lying on a beach was revolting.

Now the withdrawal symptoms were upon him. He *needed* Cannon Row as an alcoholic needs liquor. That was where he lived his life – he certainly didn't do much living in his house – and that was where, at this crucial time, he needed to be. It was the centre of things. It was where the shit was going to fly if it was going to fly. It was where he could keep track, like a missile early warning system, on Stoker.

London was quiet. He drove down the Queenstown Road, past the old Battersea power station. It was supposed to have been turned into a fun palace, then a museum, then God knew what, but nothing had been done. The old wharves were still there, the place was looking derelict. A kind of modern archaeological site.

He'd been in there a couple of times looking for suspects, but all he'd found were tramps and dossers, most of whom were too drunk to know what year it was. But there didn't seem to be anyone about on this bitter morning.

He negotiated the security gates at Cannon Row. The desk sergeant looked up as he entered the building.

'Can't keep away then, George?'

Macrae growled a greeting and went to his office. He fetched the Crime Book and flicked through the pages. Nothing of immediate interest.

He checked his messages. There was one from Norman Paston. He was reaching for the phone when Scales appeared in the doorway.

He made to walk on but Macrae looked up. Scales nodded coldly. 'I thought you were off for a few days.'

'I am.'

Stalemate.

Scales said, 'Have you seen the papers this morning? The *Chronicle*'s got a piece on a new shake-up in the Met. Apparently the Home Secretary wants it made easier to sack officers who are insubordinate or who don't do their jobs properly. And not soon enough, in my opinion.'

'I must have read a different story. Mine said it was the senior officers who were going to go if they didn't get their backsides off their chairs. But then you can never believe a blind word of what the papers say, can you, sir?' He smiled to take the edge off his words.

The Deputy Commander looked at him with loathing and went off down the corridor.

Macrae's hand went out to the phone again, then he checked. It'd be just like the bastard to come tiptoeing back to ask if he was using the bloody thing for a private call.

He left the station and drove north. Paston lived in a block of flats off Baker Street, with a TV monitor in the foyer, shatterproof glass doors, a security guard, and genuine potted plants. It was all a bit rich for Macrae's blood but Norman's boyfriends seemed to like it.

'George? What brings you here at this hour?'

'Your phone call.'

'Well, come in, come in. You know Lionel, don't you?'

Macrae had met Lionel once or twice. He was a bricklayer from Sunderland whose accent needed subtitles. He was a large, well-scrubbed young man with a single earring. One earring was supposed to be a signal that you were homosexual or heterosexual. It depended in which ear you wore it. But Macrae had never admired men in earrings and anyway he'd forgotten which ear was supposed to indicate which – so they were all dodgy to him.

Lionel was wearing jeans and a chambray shirt and looked ordinary next to Norman who wore a yellow paisley dressing-gown and Moroccan slippers. Paston noticed Macrae's inspection of his gown and said, 'Noël Coward had one just like it.'

Macrae was always a bit uneasy in the lush surroundings of Norman's flat, the heavy brocades, the overstuffed button-backed furniture in mustards and greens, the velvets, the mirrors; it was all a bit like a *fin de siècle* French brothel. Macrae had no personal knowledge of such an establishment and his own shorthand would have been 'a tart's flat in Brighton'. He wondered if Frenchy would have approved.

'Croissant, George? They're bloody good. Lionel makes them. Don't you, sweetie?'

'Maydwiswatebutteh,' Lionel said.

It took Macrae some moments to work out that what Lionel had said was 'made with sweet butter'.

'No thanks, I've had mine.'

'To business then.'

Macrae followed him into his study. There was nothing *fin de siècle* about this room. It was functional, professional, with a word processor, a modem, a fax, and filing cabinets. And it was extremely neat.

Macrae sat in a brown leather office chair and Paston went to his desk. He pulled out a sheet of paper.

'You ever heard of a villain called Jimmy Swallow?'

'No.'

'No reason why you should. He never worked in your area. He was murdered, found on Primrose Hill. It's possible Stoker was involved.'

He filled Macrae in about the attempted encroachment on Artie Gorman's patch but Macrae shook his head. 'That was never Artie's speed. I mean I knew him well enough. He wasn't above

137

nicking a few quid here and there, a bit of fraud, that sort of thing. But murder? Never.'

'From what I hear it was supposed to be in the nature of a warning. He wanted Jimmy Swallow warned off. So he gets Stoker to give him a good seeing to. Probably only supposed to break an arm. But Stoker goes too far.'

'It's all in the air, laddie. Nothing concrete.'

'Ah, but Georgie, I've got a name. There was a partner. One Mick "Toasties" Buckle. He was Swallow's partner. He'd know a lot more than he ever divulged in the first place or I'm very much mistaken.'

'I've never known you to be mistaken, Norman.' Paston frowned. 'Small joke.'

'OK, George, always warn me. I can never tell. Oh, and by the way, this isn't free. I want something in return.'

'What?'

'I hear a whisper, just the very faintest whisper, that a senior officer is on the take. I'd like the story.'

'Christ. I haven't even heard it myself. Where? The Yard?'

'I don't know. And I don't mean today, this minute. I mean when it hardens. You'll hear eventually. You always do. Then the name please, Georgie, the name.'

17

Irene held the cardboard file in her hands as though it was a bomb, which in a way it was. She was afraid of it. Of course she didn't have to open it but what would be the point of that?

She opened it.

There were over three hundred pages of neatly typed material. It looked professional.

'That's why we read it,' Juliette Simmonds had said when Irene met her. 'Usually we don't give much attention to unsolicited manuscripts unless an agent sends them. But this looked so professionally done.'

Irene had met her in the reception area of Kingswood Publishers. Miss Simmonds was tall and thin and appeared to be in her late twenties. She wore large glasses in orange frames, in an effort, Irene thought, to give her rather gaunt face some drama.

After she had expressed her shock and sadness at Grace's death, she said, 'Forgive me, but you and she must have been more like sisters than mother and daughter.'

'I had her when I was very young.'

Irene was aware that she was being studied closely and felt a touch of irritation.

'She said she had never written fiction before,' Miss Simmonds said.

'Not that I know of.'

'You weren't here then?'

'I've been living in Spain.' She put her hand out to take the manuscript.

Miss Simmonds said, 'I wish we could have made something of this. But she seemed too close to the subject. As though she was on the inside looking out.'

'I'm not sure what you mean.'

'Well . . . ' She paused as though unwilling to go on, then said, 'Well, she seemed very much on the edge. Both physically and mentally.'

'Go on.'

'I don't know how to put this without seeming to be unkind.'

'Be unkind.'

'She looked as though she'd been sleeping rough. Could that be right?'

'I don't think so.'

'It's just that her clothes were uncared for and the same could be said for herself. There was a bruise on her forehead. She kept pulling her hair over it but it was visible. And she seemed so, well, febrile is the best way I can describe it. On the edge of hysteria. And given the book's contents it was easy to see why. That's the reason I thought she was too close . . . I mean too close to be able to see the story objectively. I hope I'm wrong . . . I hope it was all in her imagination . . . '

These were the thoughts that remained with Irene all the way home. So much so that she did not have the courage to open the manuscript until she'd had a couple of large gins. The memory of Grace's suicide note was terrifyingly fresh in her mind.

The heading on the title page read:

IN THE FORESTS OF THE NIGHT
by Grace Davies

Gwen Daley lived in a garden flat in Clapham. She was lonely, but that was nothing new, she had always been lonely, for her mother had deserted her when she was very young . . .

Oh God, Irene thought, I don't want to go on with this.

But she did. It was all there, her life, her mother's life, Grace's life. It was like reading a family history written by a person you thought you knew but didn't, about lives you thought you knew but didn't. For, as she read, she began to realize how events became changed by another's perspective.

She read on and on as the hours passed. She saw herself emerge from the pages as selfish and unthinking both to her daughter and her mother. Something inside her seemed to wither and die.

By the time she reached the final chapters her psyche had twisted out of shape, and she was hunchbacked by guilt and despair and anger.

These were the chapters when 'Gwen' began her affair with 'Geoffrey'. When she suffered, martyr-like, the beatings, then the abasement by Geoffrey, the closeness, the scenes of forgiveness, the cathartic love.

And then the pastoral idyll, all passion spent, the drives in the sports car, the playfulness of the dog . . .

'A dram and a pint.'

'Grouse, Mr Macrae?' The barman asked.

'No, no, make it Glenmorangie. And a large one.' To hell with the expense, he thought.

He was in the Blind Pig in Battersea. It was early evening and business was light.

'Still very cold,' the barman said.

'Aye.'

'Hate these bloody fogs. Thought we wasn't supposed to have no more.'

Macrae grunted and took his dram and pint to a table out of sight of the fruit machine. Now he had only the sound of piped music to put up with.

He took half the Glenmorangie at a gulp, feeling the smoky fire of the Speyside malt in the back of his throat. This is what the nobs had drunk on shooting days at Morile Mhor, the great estate where his father had worked as keeper.

'Come along, Macrae,' the laird would say at the end of the last grouse drive of the day. 'Come and take a dram.'

It was a ritual. And his father would touch his cap and stand to attention and take his dram – usually in a crystal glass – while the guns gathered in small groups and unscrewed the tops of their flasks and gave themselves something to keep out the chill. Most drank Glenmorangie or Islay or one of the great single malts.

The laird always gave his father a bottle of Glenmorangie for Christmas. By the end of Boxing Day it was finished.

It was what Macrae would have drunk all the time – if he could have afforded it – and none of your supermarket muck.

He opened his briefcase, scarred and battered, a bit like

himself, and took out a copy of statements made during the investigation into the murder of James Herbert Swallow, bludgeoned to death on Primrose Hill.

There were the reports from the forensic team, the fingerprint team, the doctor who originally examined the body, statements taken by detectives, there was the post-mortem report from the government pathologist, there was a statement from the young man who had found the body when walking his dog, there were eyewitness reports of a blue Ford Escort seen near the scene . . . There was everything except the name of the person or persons who had killed him.

Nothing about Stoker.

He put these away and took out a single sheet of computer listing-paper. Michael John Buckle. There was an address in Wandsworth. Macrae glanced down the list of previous convictions. Mick Buckle had been a naughty boy in his younger days: burglary, suspicion of robbery, car theft, etc., etc. Macrae could have recited the litany blindfolded. There had been a period of youth custody. Then a year in the Scrubs. Common-law wife. Three kids.

Macrae thought that the time had come to have a word with Michael J. Buckle.

He finished his pint and drove home, ate a Cornish pasty he had bought earlier in the day and which had crumbled in its packet. It smelled awful and he doused it with Worcester sauce to kill the taste. Then he checked Buckle's address in the new phone book. The Percy Estate. SW17. Same as the one Norman Paston had given him.

Well, he was still there, but did he want to go to Wandsworth now? The Glenmorangie had changed the receptors in his mouth.

'I've got the taste, laddie,' his father used to say. And Macrae would hang around outside a pub in Morile or Inverness or wherever it was and the minutes would tick by and then the quarters and the half-hours and finally his father would stagger out and give him a bag of crisps.

Why not have a few more drinks and ring Julius and ask if Frenchy was free for the night? And see Buckle tomorrow.

The phone rang.

A woman's voice said, 'Is that Mr Macrae?'

'Yes.'

'It's Gladys.'

'Who?'

'Mrs Twyford. Eddie's wife.'

'I'm sorry. I was miles away.'

'Eddie said that to me once. He said Mr Macrae wouldn't hear him sometimes, he was so deep in thought about a case. I hope I'm not disturbing you.'

Her speech was formal, hesitant.

'That's all right. No bother. How are you, Mrs Twyford?'

'My back's not too good. But it never was. Eddie used to rub it.'

'Aye, rubbing's good for backs.' They paused. 'And apart from your back?'

'That's what I'm phoning about. You see . . . Oh, Mr Macrae, I'm so ashamed! I wouldn't ask except there's no one else, and Eddie said—'

He could hear her snuffling.

'Take it gently. What did Eddie say?'

'He used to say, "Gladys, if anything goes wrong Mr Macrae will fix it." But we never had to ask before. He thought the world of you, sir.'

'Don't call me sir.'

'I'm sorry . . . I'm very, very sorry . . . Mr Macrae, I need five hundred pounds.'

Christ, Macrae thought, not another one.

'Are you there?'

'Yes, I'm here. Listen, Mrs Twyford, I have to tell you—'

'It's five hundred and fifty, really. But I can manage the fifty. You see he wouldn't take it monthly. I been saving for my grave, next to Eddie. Oh, I know I said to him what's the use? But still . . . You can't lie next to ashes can you? If you was cremated, that is. I want to be next to him. But this other thing . . . I mean when you're dead you're dead, in my opinion. But when you're alive they can do things to you—'

'Mrs Twyford.'

'They knocked me down and took my money.'

143

'Who?'

'Them. The yobbos. That's what Eddie called them. Well, when you're dead they can't do that no more. You're safe when you're dead.'

'But what's that got to do with the five hundred pounds?'

'That's what he wants.'

'Who's he?'

'Mr Geach, the housing manager.'

'Hang on, Mrs Twyford, you're going too fast. This Mr Geach wants five hundred pounds from you, is that right? What for?'

'It's the administration costs and the stamp duty.'

'Stamp duty? You're not *buying* a house, are you? Besides . . . '

'Me buying? No, Mr Macrae. Couldn't afford to. No, it's the move to Briar. He said he could move me if the other lady don't come back from hospital. Get me away from the yobbos. I can't sleep, Mr Macrae. Not at night. There's the music all the time. So I says can I pay you monthly. I'll use my burial-fund money. Cash he says. No cheques. That's why I rung you.'

Macrae took a deep breath.

'Let me get this straight. This man Geach wants five hundred quid from you—'

'That's the admin—'

'Hang on, hang on . . . He wants five hundred quid to move you from the place you're living in to another block of flats on the estate. Is that right?'

'And the stamp duty.'

'Never mind the stamp duty!'

Macrae felt the Glenmorangie burst from his pores in sweat.

'Listen to me. Don't you give him a penny. D'you hear?'

'Yes, Mr Macrae.'

'Not a bloody penny. Just you sit tight in your wee flat and let me have a word with him. OK?'

He had considered explaining about the administration costs and the stamp duty but it would only have upset her even more. He wondered how people like Gladys Twyford survived.

'Thank you, Mr Macrae. I won't.'

He sat looking at the phone for some minutes after he had hung up. First Billy Rampton, now Gladys Twyford. To some people he must look like a bloody millionaire.

144

18

'Respect,' Stoker said. 'That's the most important thing. I mean I respect you, you respect me. Right?' He was slightly drunk.

'What about love?' Molly said. 'Where does that come in?'

'Respect *and* love. Respect . . . love . . . sex . . . '

They were naked together in the semi-darkness of Molly's room. Stoker was drinking champagne, Molly vodka. The bedroom had been decorated when Artie was alive and when each had had their own rooms. It was fluffy and girlish with a canopy over the bed and most flat spaces occupied by little china ornaments.

Stoker looked at the glass. 'Dunno why people drink the stuff. Tastes sour to me.' He poured a little champagne into Molly's navel and licked it.

'Don't. It's cold.'

'Doesn't turn you on?'

'Women don't like cold things. You know what they say about the definition of a gentleman?'

'What?'

'A man who warms his hands first.'

'Why? Oh, yeah . . . I see. Before he puts them—'

'That's it, Gary.'

'You ever done it in a swimming-pool?'

'No. Why?'

'Just wondered.' He pushed himself on to his back. 'That's why I like older women. You can talk to them about things like that.'

'Doing it in swimming-pools?'

'Yeah. You can't talk to young birds that way. They dunno what the hell you're on about. Most of them never even seen a swimming-pool. I mean a private one. Except on telly.'

145

'You like talking about sex, don't you, Gary?'

'You got any objections?'

'No.'

''Cause you like it too, don't you? But kids. What do they know? They won't do this, they won't do that. No imagination.'

She lit a cigarette and gave him a draw. 'Tell me what you want.'

He thought about it for a moment. 'I dunno, really.'

'I mean any way you like.'

'Sometimes I think there's got to be more to it.'

'Don't you like it the way it is?'

'Course I like it. It's just—'

'You're not into S&M, are you?'

'Hang on. You mean chains and things?'

'And whips and handcuffs.'

'They wear handcuffs?'

'Some of them.'

'How do you know? You been doing it like that?'

'Don't be silly.'

'With Artie? Is that what turned him on?'

'You know better than that.'

'Handcuffs!' He was silent for a moment and then said, 'You know I ain't heard nothing from Macrae.'

'What brought that on? Talking about handcuffs?'

'Dunno.'

'Nothing has to bring it on, does it? It's just there all the time. It's what's called obsessive.'

'I told you what he done to me.'

'That's all in the past, darling. I mean if we thought about the past all the time we wouldn't have a future.'

He swung his legs off the bed and sat with his back to her. 'I put the word out about him. The grasses'll do the rest. I *hate* grasses but sometimes they're useful.'

'I thought you wanted George on your side. I thought you wanted him on the payroll.'

'I thought so too at first. Not now. I want him out of the Force. I want him on his knees. I want him begging.'

His voice had a dreamy quality.

146

'You *are* obsessed.'

'You know what he did to me? He and two other coppers. They took me down to a cell—'

'You told me, Gary.'

'—and they said right, my son, we're going to give you a serious talking to. The bastards. Anyway, don't fucking interrupt me! If I want to tell you a thousand times I'll do it. OK?'

'Why do we always have to talk about him? Macrae this and Macrae that. Even here in the bedroom when we're making love. I don't like talking about him any time, specially not now.'

'What sort of talk do you want then?'

She stubbed out her cigarette angrily and said, 'Any sort of talk where Macrae's name doesn't come up and what he did to you and what you're going to do to him.'

'You want to talk about sex? That's all you can think of. Twenty-four hours a day.'

He got up and began to dress.

'Where you going? You're not leaving me again, are you?'

'I'm going to that expensive fish place in Lisson Grove. Get us a couple of fish suppers. Get a video. Something good. *Scarface*. Something like that. OK? I got permission?'

'The last time you went down to that place you never came back.'

'You're not my bleedin' mother! But you sound like her all right.'

He threw his shirt across the room, pulled open a drawer, and got out a fresh one.

'Gary, I'm sorry. I didn't mean it.'

'You rather fancy him, don't you?'

'Who?'

'Macrae. You do, don't you?'

'Don't be silly!'

He was buttoning his shirt and he stopped. 'You know what I'd like to do to him?'

'What?'

'I'd like to—'

He paused, savouring the moment, and again there was the dreamy quality in his voice.

147

'Kill him?' she said.

'Yeah . . . Yeah . . . I'd really like that.'

Leo Silver was tired and cold and hungry – he hadn't eaten tor eight hours – and he was also sore and stiff. It was dark and his eyes felt heavy. As Zoe would have said in circumstances like these: 'Leo, I'm not having a very nice time.'

If he hadn't felt so cold he would have been asleep and that was the reason he hadn't switched on the car heater. Warmth equalled sleep and all his attention needed to be focused on Molly Gorman's house.

He'd been sitting in his Golf, on and off but mainly on, since the day before. It was now night.

And he was missing – very badly – Zoe and his bed and a bath and a drink.

And he was missing Macrae and Eddie Twyford.

Usually the three of them would have been on a job like this and the time would have passed punctuated by a series of arguments between Macrae and Eddie about which was the best way to get from Hampstead to Bethnal Green or where to park in the West End, arguments that were irritating while they lasted but which he would have loved to hear just then.

But there never would be an argument now because Eddie was dead and Macrae was half-way down the tube and Leo didn't know, in his cold and depressed state, whether he felt like staying on in the police.

If they busted Macrae he would think seriously of getting out.

It wasn't as though he supported Macrae's methods but there was something about the big thief taker that made Leo admire him in spite of himself. It was the same kind of admiration he might have had for a traction engine or a steam locomotive or a wily old buffalo.

Suddenly the image of the buffalo put another image into his mind. He had once been to a bullfight and had been moved at the tragedy of the bull and not the *faena* as a whole. Now for a second or two he saw Macrae as a huge Miura with the pic holes in his shoulders and the banderillas hanging down the blood-soaked neck, head lowered, waiting for the last act. And for the first time he saw him as a figure of tragedy.

With him gone there would only be people like Wilson and Scales and he wasn't sure he could bear that. He knew – in a moment of instantaneous nostalgia – that he was never going to feel the same about the Met again.

Scales had been looking for him for the past few days but he'd managed to avoid him. Even Wilson had come looking for him on Scales' behalf.

He wouldn't be able to avoid him much longer. Anyway, Macrae's leave ran out in a few days and then all hell would break loose.

When he had discussed this with Zoe she had said, 'Leo, you've got to keep your head down otherwise you'll get sucked into this.'

And he had replied, 'It's far too late for that. Anyway that's all the senior ranks ever do. They keep their heads down. That's how Scales has got where he is – by keeping his head down.'

The door of Molly Gorman's house opened. Light fell on the steps and he saw Stoker in silhouette. He watched him get into his Rolls and drive away.

It took several minutes for anyone to answer Leo's ring on the doorbell. The lights in the house were on and he could hear the beat of music. Then the door opened and Molly stood in the hall.

'Yes?'

The light was behind her and all he could see was the shape of a woman under a clinging, filmy robe.

'Detective Sergeant Silver,' he said, showing her his warrant card.

'Silver? Oh, yes, you're George Macrae's sergeant, aren't you?'

'That's right.'

She made no move.

'I'd like to talk to you.'

'I'm just about to have a bath.'

'It's important.'

'Is it about George?'

'Yes it is.'

'Well, there's nothing I can do about—'

'And it's about Stoker.'

'What's Gary been up to?'

'I think you know.'

'I don't want to talk to you.'

'And it's about you.'

'Me?'

'I think I'd better come in, don't you?'

She backed away and led him into the flock-Tretchikoff drawing-room. He was able to see her more clearly. Her hair was loose and rumpled and she had nothing on under her robe. Each curve and hollow of her amply proportioned body was plainly visible and Silver, who had of late lived a celibate existence, was moved by the sight of it all.

She did not ask him to sit down but waited for him to speak.

He said, 'That was Stoker leaving, wasn't it?' She nodded. 'I've been waiting a long time. I wanted to speak to you alone.'

'Well, you'd better make it snappy. He's only gone for fish and chips.'

'OK.' Silver took a deep breath and plunged into the murky waters of coercion. 'It's about George Macrae.'

'I thought you said it was about me.'

'We'll get to you.'

She lit a cigarette and pushed back her heavy hair. He knew she was in her forties but even so she had something.

'I understand George Macrae borrowed some money from your late husband.'

She eyed him stonily. 'What about it?'

'I want to know if it's true and how much.'

'He never discussed his business dealings with me.'

'I'll bet.'

'It's true.'

'OK, well let's pretend it *is* the truth. In that case you're being done by your boyfriend. He's taking your money.'

'Gary's my business manager.'

Silver digested this piece of unlikely information.

'I've never met Stoker. Sorry – Gary. But I've seen his file and I wouldn't have immediately placed him in a commercial advisory capacity.'

'I don't give a damn where you'd place him. Listen, I've no time—'

'That's only part one. The word's out on the street and my guv'nor won't like it.'

'George never sent you. He'd never send a young lad on something like this.' Then she said, 'You're Jewish, aren't you?'

'No one's perfect.'

'I mean what's a Jew doing in the Met?'

'I must introduce you to my parents.'

'Artie was a Jew. He'd never have gone into the police.'

'As I recall his file Artie went into all sorts of other things, most of which were illegal or unethical.'

'That was long ago. Before we were married.'

'I want you to stop Stoker. I want whatever you're holding – an IOU or whatever it is – destroyed. I want this forgotten. OK?'

'You must be out of your mind coming here and demanding things like that.'

'Listen—'

'No, you listen. I've known Macrae for years. I tolerated him because Artie had a soft spot for him. But I hate coppers. And Macrae crawled to him for money!'

'Macrae never crawled to anyone and you know it!'

'I tell you he was desperate!'

'I know the guv'nor a lot better than you. He never crawled to anyone, least of all to some bent little bookie, or for that matter a cowboy like Stoker.'

'You watch your mouth!'

Suddenly Silver lost his cool. 'You brought up the old days. OK. So here's a little history lesson.' He pulled from an inside pocket a folded sheet of paper. He knew most of it off by heart but reading it seemed more dramatic. 'Molly Anne Gorman, 43, née Slattery. Convicted of soliciting, shoplifting, possession of cannabis, drunk and disorderly—'

'That's a lie. They fitted me up on that one. Anyway so bloody what? All this was a long time ago and Artie knew all about it.'

'But what about Stoker? Does he know?'

'You're kidding. Course he knows. I told him.' She laughed. 'You really think you can come here with stuff like that and hold it over me?'

'OK. Try these names. Hadfield.'

He looked up and saw her eyes narrow.

'Leask.'

She jerked slightly.

'Prothero. Macklin . . . You want me to go on?'

Very slowly she sat down in one of the easy chairs.

'That was years and years ago,' she said. 'I was only a kid then.'

'You were eighteen.'

'Only a kid.'

'Eighteen isn't a kid. You know what you're doing at eighteen. You gave these villains to the law, didn't you? To Detective Chief Superintendent Bulloch at the Yard, to be exact. You were a grass, an informer, the lowest of the low.'

She had looked away and was staring at the wall as though Silver had left the room.

Softly she said, 'I had to.'

'Why did you have to?'

'Why does anyone have to? Money, of course.'

'Drugs?'

She nodded. 'Bulloch made a deal.'

'How could an eighteen-year-old—?'

'Because I was Jack Slattery's daughter.'

'Jack Slattery.' The name jolted him. It was a well-known name to every copper. 'He killed two policemen in Shoreditch. Escaped after a few years and killed again. The police shot him dead in the West End somewhere. Is that the Jack Slattery?'

She looked towards the door. 'He was part òf the Krays' scene. The East End gangs.'

'So you were right at the centre of things. A young kid. Jack Slattery's daughter. They could talk in front of you. Safe as a house. Well, well, well. And that's where Stoker comes from.'

'I know.'

'I mean that's his background. The macho man from White-chapel and points East.'

'Yeah.'

'You know the other name I've got on the sheet?'

She nodded again. 'How was I to know I'd have an affair with his son more than twenty years later? I mean the name didn't mean anything to me at first. There're lots of people called Stoker. It was just things he said. Names he mentioned. Then I knew. But by that time it was too late.'

'What d'you think Stoker would do if he knew you'd sent his dad away to die in the nick?'

'Christ you'd never—! I mean—!'

'Do you know the phrase *quid pro quo*? It means you scratch my back and I'll scratch yours.'

19

It was early evening and Macrae was driving home from Wandsworth hoping that the smell of the flat he had just visited would not have permeated his clothing. If the smell was anything to go by you could have scraped the cooking fat from the walls with the back of a knife.

The fact was it had been a partly wasted journey. Macrae had wearily climbed to the ninth floor of the tower block on the council estate – the lifts, naturally, were out of order – only to meet a man who did not know anything at all.

Literally.

His common-law wife, in her late twenties, looked to be in her late forties. Her two children appeared to Macrae to have stepped from the pages of *Our Mutual Friend*, a copy of which he had been reading for the past couple of months. These with their big eyes and thin bodies were what he imagined the offspring of the river rats to have been like.

The three of them watched him with a kind of dull incuriousness as he asked if Mick Buckle was there.

Mrs Buckle, doughy and overweight, said, 'Where else would he be?'

She took Macrae through to the bedroom, where a man was sitting in a wheelchair – although sitting wasn't quite the word Macrae would have used. He was strapped to the chair in case he toppled sideways on to the floor. His head lolled on his shoulder as though he had muscular dystrophy. He was facing the window and his eyes, though open, appeared to be dead.

'There's a gentleman to see you, Mick.' It was said more as a kind of tired litany than for any sense it made. There was no reaction.

'Does he know I'm here?' Macrae said.

'He doesn't know nothing. Brain damage.'

'What happened?'

'Hit and run.'

'I didn't know,' Macrae said. 'It's not in his file.'

She made no response.

He stood looking down at the relic in the wheelchair.

'And nothing? No speech, no reactions?'

'Not a bleedin' thing. You might just as well put him in a box.'

Macrae blenched inwardly at the callousness of her remark but after a moment he thought: *What if you had to live with this day after day after day?*

'Mick's like a vegetable.' As she spoke she wiped her husband's mouth. She did it automatically as though it was a gesture she had made ten thousand times before.

Her movement caused the air in the room to stir and Macrae, who had been trying not to notice the rank smell of drains and frying, felt his gorge rise. The two kids were standing in the doorway looking at him.

'When did it happen?' he asked.

'I lost count,' she said. 'Feels like a million years.'

He had a suspicious thought. 'Was it about the time of the Jimmy Swallow murder?'

'Some time about then.'

'He and Jimmy were trying to set up a gambling operation in Camden, weren't they?'

'Something like that.'

'Where did someone like Mick get the finance from for a job like that?'

'I dunno. He never spoke about his work. He was always on the phone, though. There may have been another bloke with cash.'

'And the accident, the hit and run, happened around the time of the murder? Before or after?'

'After.'

'Just after? A month after?'

'I dunno. Maybe a month.'

'He'd seen the police by then? I mean he'd been interviewed about Jimmy Swallow's murder?'

155

'Yeah.'

'Was anyone ever arrested for the hit and run?'

'No one ever said.'

'You'd have been told. Does the name Stoker mean anything to you? Gary Stoker?'

He suddenly saw her expression change. He looked down at Buckle. The thin film of froth had returned to his lips but otherwise he was unchanged.

'Do you know Stoker?'

'Listen, I got the kids to see to.'

'You do, don't you? D'you think he was the hit and run driver?'

'Please,' the woman said. 'I answered hundreds of questions. It ain't got anyone anywhere.'

'But did anyone ask you about Stoker?'

She shook her head.

'Listen to me for a wee moment. Your husband's been totally wrecked. His friend Swallow was killed. Hit with a tyre lever. We think Stoker killed him. And now my guess is that it was Stoker who ran him down in case Mick ever came forward to name him as Jimmy's killer. You want someone like that left to run around London like Attila the Hun?'

'Who?'

'Never mind, just think about what he did.'

'I got enough problems without—'

'Stoker.'

'Yeah, without Stoker.'

'The police'll protect you.'

'That's what the coppers said to Mick before the accident.'

'All right,' Macrae said. 'I'll leave you to think about it. But I'll be back.' At the door, he said, 'By the way, why is he called "Toasties"?'

'I dunno,' she said. 'I never asked.'

Now, driving home through the misty winter night on the south side of the river, Macrae was caught in a dilemma. If it was Stoker then he had a duty to pass his suspicions on. He began to ponder on an extremely complex double-play: what if he had been suspicious of Stoker right from the start as the killer of Jimmy Swallow? After all, he had arrested him and interviewed him in

156

Hackney when he'd assaulted the PC. Take it a step further. What if he had used Artie as a stalking-horse to get at Stoker? Of course it would only work if he did get Stoker. But it might be worth a try. Cloud the issue. Muddy the waters. He might even come out of it looking good. He'd have to go back to Buckle's grisly flat. Next time he wouldn't leave without a statement.

He found himself in Clapham High Street and on an impulse turned towards Linda's house. He owed her an apology for the other night. He parked and went up the front steps. The flat seemed to be in darkness. He looked up at Leitman's flat. It too was in darkness. Coincidence?

He rang her bell then began knocking on the front door. It was loud in the quiet street. A woman's voice below him said, 'Excuse me, who do you want?'

'Mrs Macrae.'

'She isn't here.' She came up the steps. 'Is that Mr Macrae? It's Irene Isard.'

'Oh, aye. I was passing. I thought I'd call in.'

'I'm afraid Linda's away.'

'Away?' He made it sound as though it was a criminal offence.

'Only for a day or two. She went up to Scotland.'

He frowned. 'I've never known her go to Scotland. Whatever for?'

'I think it's just a little break, Mr Macrae.'

'Oh, well . . .'

'It's a pity you've come all this way for nothing. Can I give you a cup of coffee?'

Macrae had had enough of people for one night. 'No, I must be getting—'

'I'm just making one.' She moved so that he was now between her and the open door. 'Or a drink. That would be better wouldn't it at this time? I know I could do with one.'

Almost imperceptibly, she had been moving him towards the flat doorway.

He shrugged mentally. An attractive woman . . . a drink . . . warmth . . .

'Of course you will,' she said.

He paused, but only fractionally. 'Aye. That would be nice.'

He was taken with her flat. He liked the colours and the warmth. He wondered why he'd never been able to get his own flat looking like this.

'I went to Spain a couple of times,' he said, 'but it's all concrete now.'

'We made it like that, now we despise it.' She gave him a whisky.

'Glenmorangie!'

'The man I . . . my husband – my late husband, that is – used to drink it. You'd know it, of course.'

'It's the one I prefer. Is something wrong?'

She indicated her eyes. 'No, no. I've been cutting up onions.' There was a pause. She sipped her whisky and said, 'That's a lie. It's just that the day has been . . . well, bloody awful.'

He sat back and thought: someone else with a bloody awful day behind them, and wondered if she, too, was about to touch him for money.

'I've spent it with a friend. She's been having a bad time.'

He nodded, trying to look interested.

'I've been with her all day. It's rather sad, really.'

'D'you mind if I light up?' He held up a packet.

'Please. I like the smell of a cigar.'

He lay back, drawing on the thin panatella and sipping the Glenmorangie, and let her words wash over him.

'Do you know much about battered women?'

'Me?' He said it as though her question had been an accusation. 'No, no, I've come across cases but not many.'

'Well, my friend comes from a background of violence. It started with her father. He battered her mother. And she – my friend that is – lived with her mother in a refuge for battered women when she was a young girl. She was frightened to death of her father. So it was only natural that when she could escape from her family, she did.

'She had a child. It wasn't as though she was leaving a baby though. The girl was in her mid-teens and—'

'You've lost me,' Macrae said.

'Oh, I'm sorry. My friend had a daughter. When she was about fifteen she left home and went to live in a squat and wouldn't . . . *would not* . . . come home even though her mother

158

tried and tried. That's the point I'm trying to make. Because when my friend couldn't get her daughter to return home . . . I mean she was on drugs and everything . . . and the men . . . God, it was really bad!'

'You seem very close.'

'Well, she was my . . . goddaughter.'

'What's the girl's name?' Macrae said.

'Gwen. Anyway, Gwen finally killed herself. She was being battered too.'

They stared at each other. Macrae had heard many stories told about 'friends'. He wondered if this was another, but he was so bloody tired and mixed up and concerned with his own affairs that he didn't give much of a toss one way or the other.

'They say some women subconsciously want to be battered,' she said.

'I've heard of it. I've never come across it.'

'My friend's mother . . . she was a strange woman. She seemed to prefer the rough side of life. She came from quite a good family but she married a warrant officer who eventually became a major. He put on a good accent and pretended to be someone he wasn't. Sometimes my friend wondered if her mother wasn't one of these women. Do you think it's possible for that sort of thing to skip a generation?'

'God knows.'

'My friend wondered, you know, if it hadn't reappeared in Grace. The one who killed herself.'

'I thought you said her name was Gwen.'

'Yes, yes, it is Gwen. What did I say?'

'Grace.'

'Did I? I wonder why?'

Macrae was becoming enmeshed in something he didn't need. He finished the drink and mashed out his cigar and began the small movements and rearrangements of clothes and limbs that presaged departure.

But she was up in a flash with the bottle and the taste was there and he thought, what the hell, it was free. All he had to do was lend half an ear.

'So anyway,' Irene continued. 'My friend's daughter, Gwen, got herself into a situation where she too was being battered. And she killed herself. But then a strange thing happened. She'd written a book – a novel. Except it wasn't really a novel, it was just what had happened to her and her family. And the manuscript of this novel popped up after her death. And my friend's been reading it. That's why she wanted me to come over and be with her.'

'Oh, aye,' Macrae said, feeling the whisky spread out into his muscles.

'It's the most terrible indictment of her mother. She says in her novel that her mother abandoned her, didn't love her. It's a terrible thing to read, Mr Macrae.'

'I suppose it is.' His own children passed briefly before his mind's eye and he wondered what kind of novel they would write about him.

'She phoned me up and she was quite distraught and I went to keep her company. And, well, we had a good old cry.'

Macrae stared at Irene and thought: She's lying, she'd never use a phrase like that if she was telling the truth. A good old cry? Sounded like someone who'd gone to a weepie at the pictures. But he found he didn't care.

'Have you got any children? Oh, yes, of course, you have. Linda told me. You've got a daughter.'

'I've got two daughters. And a son. Different wives.'

'You'll know how my friend feels then. It's the guilt. It's terrible.'

'Aye. That's the point about having kids. Doesn't matter what you do for them – if something goes wrong you're to blame. And there's no escaping the guilt.'

He said it so forcefully that she blinked at him.

'You know then how she must be feeling.'

'I can guess.'

Irene rose and gave herself another drink and, without asking, poured one for Macrae. He did not demur. Manna did not often fall like this.

What a different scene this was from the one he had just left. That was true *underclass*; this, on the other hand, was what he could do with a bit of. Warmth. Colour. Comfort. An attractive woman pouring generous amounts of Glenmorangie into splendid cut-glass tumblers.

He came out of his reverie and saw her staring at him expectantly. What the hell had she asked him?

Her face softened and she said, 'You look all in.'

'Well, some of the work gets you down a bit.'

'I'm sure it does. You see people in the raw.'

'Aye, that's the truth.'

'I wish I'd known you when . . . when Gwen was alive. You might have been able to stop things.'

'How?'

'Well, warn the man off.'

'The police can't go round sticking in their noses. No, no, we can only act on a complaint or after a crime's been committed.'

'By then it's often too late.'

He wasn't going to get into that argument. 'Why didn't she complain if she was being battered? There are women's organizations. You mentioned one yourself: refuges. Was she married to him?'

'No.'

'Then she could have kicked him out.'

'She wanted to redeem him.'

'She *what*?'

'She wrote it in her book. She said she only felt alive *after* he had beaten her. When he was begging her forgiveness. She said that was the only time in her life she really felt needed and wanted and above all loved.' She paused. 'Sorry.' She dabbed at her eyes. 'When my friend read this out to me it was hard to bear.'

Macrae could take no more. He stood up. 'People are responsible for their own lives,' he said. 'The trouble is the nanny state has emasculated us.'

She stood up too. 'Are you saying she could have stopped him by acting for herself?' Her voice had become sharp. 'Doing what? Battering him back? Killing him?'

'If it came to that. People kill each other for lesser reasons.'

'You mean self-defence?'

'The law would have been on her side. But it would have had to be in the heat of the moment. You can't plan it. You can't wait till he's asleep and stab him or take a brick to his head. The courts don't like that. They call it premeditated.'

'And you're saying that killing someone is better than the police having a quiet word beforehand?'

'We're not doctors. We don't go in for preventative medicine. We can tell you how to lock your houses and your cars and not to walk alone in dark streets, but after that it's up to you. And if you can't manage it we're here to pick up the pieces.'

'You make us sound irresponsible.'

'Not all, just some of you. Like your friend.'

'How do you mean?'

'Well, she did abandon her daughter, didn't she? Even if she rationalizes it. Good God, the girl was only fifteen! You dinna know you're born when you're fifteen.'

'What should she have done, then?' Her voice sounded hoarse with emotion.

'She should have been there. That's all we can do: just *be* there – in case. Your friend wasn't. And her daughter killed herself. Goodnight, and thanks for the whisky.'

20

Stoker had had a big night. A real blinder. He couldn't even remember half of it. As he drove home to Gospel Oak he got flashes of the action and even though his head throbbed and was painful and his eyes hurt and he felt sick, and even though he knew he was going to feel worse before he felt better – in spite of all these caveats – he'd had a brilliant time.

He had started off for the fish place in Lisson Grove, just as he'd told Molly he would, but then, half-way there, he'd decided he didn't want fish and chips or a video or Molly.

So he'd cancelled the fish and chips and put Molly on hold – he loved that phrase – and he'd gone zooming up West in the Roller. He'd visited a couple of clubs but he hadn't seen any familiar faces and anyway parking a Rolls in the West End these days was no picnic. You couldn't leave it in the street in case the yobbos scratched it or slashed the tyres so you had to find good security, and that took time.

Sometimes he didn't know what things were coming to.

So anyway . . . he'd ended up in the Goodwood. He'd looked round for Macrae but the bastard wasn't there; which was quite right because the bastard had no right to be there since he wasn't a member. But the word was out on him and it was just a matter of time before he came crawling to Stoker. Just a matter of time. Still, Stoker didn't want to meet him socially in a place like this. He wasn't absolutely one hundred per cent certain of Macrae even now.

The shithead.

Anyway he'd had a couple of drinks and a few games of kalooki and a few more drinks and he'd mixed with some of the hardest men in the business.

The real cream of the crop.

These were men who thought nothing of cleaning out whole wings of country houses, or busting open security vans; men who'd done their bird in Strangeways and Maidstone and in the high-security nicks on the Isle of Wight.

Aristocrats.

He'd stayed in the club standing his round and flashing his wedge – and he was glad to see it compared well with the wedges of the hard men – till closing time around three-thirty. Then he'd gone home with Terry someone, who'd been inside for armed robbery, and there had been more drinking in his flat in Harlesden and his wife or his girlfriend had rung up a friend and they'd had a party which had ended up four in a bed.

Then Stoker had been sick and passed out – the hallmark of a really good evening.

Now it was the middle of the day and he was feeling terrible. But he believed in the old saying: the worse the hangover the better the time.

The only thing he hadn't had was a bit of a barney. He liked that. In the early days it had occurred at football matches. You took along a club or a chain and someone shouted 'Wheeeeey Chelsea!' and it didn't matter who you were for – you weren't for anybody really, only come for a bit of fun – and you hit him in the face and then it started.

Good days.

The moment he opened the front door he knew something was wrong. A chair in the hall was lying on its side. He looked into the sitting-room. Molly's collection of leather-look display books was spilled on the floor, pictures hung awry.

'Molly!'

He ran upstairs. She was in the bedroom. Here too the pictures were disturbed.

She was sitting at the dressing-table applying make-up to a long scratch down the side of one cheek.

'What the hell happened?' Stoker said.

'Where were you?'

'Never mind that now. What happened here?'

'What d'you think? What's it look like?' Her tone was angry, bitter.

'It looks like we was burgled.'

'Clever boy.'

'Don't get sarky with me! I said what the hell happened?'

'And don't use that tone with me. I'm not one of your little tarts. I suppose that's where you've been all night. With one of your tarts!'

Stoker's head seemed about to burst apart. He sat down on the bed and said softly, 'You better tell me or I'll mark you.'

'We had a visit. That's all. While you were out gallivanting. Christ, you need your head read. You make threats and cause trouble and when the time comes where are you?'

'Threats? Who'd I threaten?'

'Who the hell d'you think? George Macrae, you silly bugger.'

Stoker experienced two simultaneous emotions: blazing anger and chilly apprehension. The delights of the night before faded. The headache grew suddenly worse. 'OK . . . OK . . . tell me what happened.'

'Well, all he had to do was wait for you to go, didn't he? You never think of consequences. That's where you're different from Artie. He was always thinking.'

'Spare me the fucking lecture!'

'Well, you won't be told. I mean all he did was sit in his car and wait for you to leave the house. And if you'd come back like you said you would none of this would have happened.'

'But – you mean he robbed us?'

'Course he didn't.'

Stoker's mind was cloudy. But at last he was able to collect his thoughts. 'Jesus! The tapes!'

He ran into the spare bedroom and one look was enough. A large oil-painting of African elephants had been thrown on to the bed and the wall safe, which it had been hiding, was open. He could see boxes of jewellery and bundles of ten- and twenty-pound notes in rubber bands, but no tape.

Molly stood in the doorway. 'He made me, Gary. Look what he did to my face.'

'Get out of my way!'

He ran downstairs and out of the french windows that led into the garden. He ran – ignoring his throbbing head – up the path to the garden office. The door was ajar. Drawers had been opened, their contents spilled out on to the floor.

'This one's gone too!' he shouted. 'And he's torn the page from the ledger!' He ran back to the house. Molly had come downstairs and he caught her by the wrist.

'You're hurting me!'

'I'll break your arm if you don't shut up. Tell me exactly what happened.'

It was soon told. An hour after he'd left Macrae arrived at the front door, forced his way in, made her give up the master tape *and* the copy. He had threatened to hurt her if she didn't co-operate and indeed had done so just, as he put it, to show willing.

Stoker stood at the windows, looking out but seeing nothing.

'He's too much for you to handle, Gary. Leave him.'

'Too much? You know what he did to me?'

'You told me.'

'Shut your mouth.'

'You want my advice, don't mix it with Macrae. You'll lose.'

'You think so?'

'I'm sure.'

'You rotten bitch.' He stood over her and she tensed in case he hit her. But his face filled with contempt and disgust. 'Look at you. When you haven't got your make-up on you could be my mother. Christ, I dunno what I saw in you.'

'I'll tell you what you saw: money, lots of it. And clothes. And an expensive car. And an available body. That's what you saw. And you had it all. Except you decided to mix it with Macrae.'

The word 'Macrae' was Pavlovian and activated something inside Stoker's aching head. He pushed Molly out of his way and ran down the front steps to the Rolls. From the back he pulled out a tyre lever but instead of getting into the Rolls he unlocked a small Mercedes parked near by – Molly's car. Macrae might know the Roller but he didn't know the Merc.

He shot off down the street in the swirling fog and began to thread his way through Camden towards Macrae's house in Battersea.

'*Muh pud prik,*' Harold Marshall said. 'Pork fried with hot chillies. Does that appeal? Or . . . ' he looked down the menu. '*Kai pud prik.* Chicken fried with hot chillies.'

He knew she knew what he was doing but she didn't seem to react.

'Or one could have *gung pud prik* – prawns cooked with chillies.

166

I wonder if those are the long thin prawns or the short fat ones. Which do you like?'

He looked slyly over the menu at her. She raised her own eyes and he flinched and looked away. It was difficult to meet those eyes. They had changed. They lay deep in her head, glowing redly. They made him uneasy, restless. It was as though, for a moment, blinds had been lifted on an inner world that frightened him in its unfamiliar intensity. He wasn't used to looking in people's eyes and finding that. Briefly he was sorry he had brought her.

It would have been hard to refuse her. She had walked into the Zanzibar at lunchtime and found him with a G and T in his hand. She had stood in the darkened room and reminded him of his offer of lunch.

'At the Thai,' he had said. 'Of course I remember. A libation first?' He touched his silvery hair. But she said she would have wine with her lunch, if that was in order.

'Absolutely.'

He was dressed much the same way as he had been on their first meeting. He flushed with pleasure as he took her arm to cross the road. He pressed firmly through the heavy wool of her coat and found the flesh beneath. He squeezed. She did not respond, but neither did she reject him.

Nothing like this had happened to Harold Marshall for a long time. His wife had died more than twenty years before and his pickings had been slender since then. No, not slender, bloody nearly zero. There had been a black cleaning lady whom he had inveigled back to his flat and whom he had paid, and there had been an elderly friend of his dead wife who had made it easy for him and then talked of marriage.

It hadn't been for want of trying, though. The problem was, he supposed, a universal one: older women did not appeal to him but he did not seem to be able to interest the younger ones.

There had been times in the past when his desperation had reached the point of wanting to buy a woman, a tart, and several times he had set off for the West End to find one.

But the streets seemed devoid of tarts. Perhaps he was looking in the wrong places but it was apparently telephone numbers in phone boxes now and he didn't like the idea of walking into an unknown flat by himself.

He'd seen reports on television of whores at King's Cross

Station, so he'd gone there. But Harold was fastidious and timid. The women, most of whom seemed drunk or high on drugs, scared him. The thought of Aids scared him. He longed for the old days when comfortable-looking women in high heels and coats stood in the darkness of shop doorways and said: 'Looking for a nice time, love?'

Now it was thigh-length boots and rubber and doing it in parked cars or derelict sites where discarded syringes glittered in the trampled weeds.

As he guided Irene to a table he felt his spirits – and what juices remained in his body – begin their upward flow, as though in a springtime long ago.

Then, for the first time, with his sly mention of *prik* this and *prik* that, he had looked over the menu directly into her eyes, and seen, well, to be frank he didn't know what it was, but it had made him uneasy.

'I don't care,' she said. 'You order.'

He made much of that. Then there was the ceremony of the wine; the Niersteiner. Was the temperature quite right? He drank thirstily. The wine on top of the G and Ts brought his face out in a military flush.

He started to relax. Her eyes no longer bothered him quite so much. God, she was a sexy piece. Just the way he liked them. Big breasted, white skinned. He visualized her with her clothes off eating the Thai food, sucking the long, greasy prawns. Keep that image, he thought, and you won't have a failure.

He put his foot out to touch hers and spoke quickly about the army days as though to cover the act. She did not reply. Hardly listened.

Abruptly she broke straight across him and said, 'Tell me about Gerald.'

He chewed a piece of fried pork and smiled hesitantly. 'What do you want to know?'

'Tell me about his women.'

'His women?'

'Is he married? Does he have girlfriends?'

'Why?'

'I'm interested in him.'

'Why?'

168

'I'm a sociologist, in a way.'

'What's Gerald—?'

'His looks for one thing. He looks like an albino.'

'God, don't ever call him that! He hates that.'

She ignored him. 'His height for another. He's short. Then the car and the dog. I wondered if he was a type, that's all.'

He drank more wine. There was something weird about Irene. No matter. If she wanted to talk about Gerald he'd talk about Gerald. He'd talk about anything, Christian Science, Hitler, the balance of payments, any bloody thing as long as she'd lie down for him and open her legs.

'Gerald,' he said, and lit a cigarette. 'Well that's quite an interesting subject, sociologically speaking.'

'Do you think he's a sociopath?'

'A what?'

'Is he mental, deranged?'

'Now hang on a sec.'

'You've known him since he was a child, haven't you?'

'Yes, but—'

'Well, is he a sadist, do you think? Is he a masochist? In other words, is he a bloody loony?'

Other patrons looked towards them and Marshall lowered his eyes.

'My dear girl, you—'

'Come on, Harold. What's his relationship with women? What turns him on? Violence? Start with his mother. Mavis, you said her name was.'

If he didn't she might become more strident.

He said, 'Gerald was afraid of her. She was his mother *and* his father. She was tough. Lots of people were afraid of her. I was myself at times. A mannish sort of woman. I called her bossy-boots, but only to myself. Don't mind admitting it.'

'We're talking about Gerald, not you.'

'I'm just trying to explain.'

'Was she violent with him?'

'Well . . . yes . . . I suppose you could say she was. But I'm not sure I'd use the word "violent". Strict. I mean she didn't stand any nonsense. She used to slap his face if he was what she called "cheeky". I was sorry for the little chap. I suppose that's why I eventually took him into the business. Of course he's damned good too.'

'You mean she hit him when he was small?'

'When he was small. When he was a teenager. She used to slap him even when he was grown up. In the office. I saw her.'

'What about his relationship with other women? Girls.'

He looked down at his plate. 'He had one once with a much older woman. I don't think I should be talking about it. It's his business.'

'Sociologists are like doctors,' she said.

He pressed her foot and she let it remain where it was for a moment, then withdrew it.

'I don't suppose it would go any further,' he said.

She pushed her foot back against his. His hand shook as he lit another cigarette.

'Well, he had an altercation with her.'

'Altercation? What's that mean?'

'He hit her. I suppose you could say he beat her up. God knows why. Anyway she called the police. But finally she wouldn't go on with it so they didn't charge him. I suppose she was too embarrassed. I mean he'd been living with her. She was over forty. Had a son older than Gerald.'

'How old was he?'

'Seventeen.'

'And then . . . '

'Then?'

Her foot touched his ankle.

'Well, he once . . . I don't know the truth of it . . . but it was said he'd tried to force himself on a customer in an empty flat. She came into the office and complained. But she was known in the district as a bit of . . . well, not a tart exactly, but someone who was of easy virtue. Yes, I think that's the phrase.'

'I wonder why he does it.'

'I know one thing. He's got a terrific temper. He doesn't like being contradicted. Gets that from Mavis.'

'He doesn't sound a very nice man.'

'Gerald's all right. Bloody good at selling, I can tell you that.'

He paid and they stood on the pavement.

'Tell Gerald I'd like to see him,' she said.

'Why?'

'There's a tap leaking.'

'Probably needs a washer.' He took her arm. 'My flat's only round the corner,' he said.

'What?'

'I thought you and I . . . you know, perhaps a Drambuie. Coffee.'

'I've got things to do,' she said.

'Hang on . . . hang on . . . '

'I've got to find an ironmonger's.' She tried to free her arm.

'You can't just leave me like this.'

'I can do anything I please.' She pulled away. 'You're a dirty old man.'

His face became blotchy. Other women had called him that.

'You bitch!'

She turned and walked away along the pavement. He watched the sway of her hips. He saw her naked. He saw her dimpled buttocks stiffen and relax with every step. He felt like crying.

'Have you been avoiding me, Sergeant?' Scales was standing at Leo's desk.

'No, sir.'

'I've left you messages. Mr Wilson tells me he gave you a message himself to report to me.'

'Things were coming to a head, sir.'

'Oh?' He bent close to Leo.

'It looks as though the information was wrong, sir.' This was said in an undertone.

'Wrong?' Scales frowned.

'My information is that the . . . uh . . . the transaction never took place. That it was a set-up. Someone was trying to put the knife in, sir.'

Scales looked thunderous. 'You'd better come into my office right away. We can't talk here.'

Scales turned and marched through the big CID office.

As he did so Leo's phone rang.

A woman's voice said, 'You know who's speaking?'

He had been speaking to her earlier that afternoon. 'Yes. I know.'

'No names, then.'

'OK.'

Scales had paused at the door and was looking at Leo who placed a hand over the receiver and said, 'I'll be right with you, sir.'

Scales nodded briskly and marched on.

'Sorry,' Leo said. 'I had to speak to someone.'

'You taping this?'

'Absolutely not. What happened?'

Without mentioning Stoker by name, Molly gave him an edited version.

'And the tapes?'

'Burnt.'

'Good. Listen, why did you bring, you know . . . into it?'

'The big man?'

'Yes. Why not keep it anonymous?'

'Don't talk soft. I had to have someone do the deed, didn't I?'

'You could have said it was me.'

'You?'

The way she said it annoyed Leo.

'Yes. Me.'

'He'd never have believed it.'

Leo swallowed his pride. 'All right, so—'

'Wait. That's not what I'm ringing about. He's gone after the big man.'

'When?'

'About an hour ago.'

'Why didn't you call me?'

'I tried to call him first. Anyway you weren't in.'

'OK. Thanks. And I mean it.'

'I don't want your bloody thanks. Whatever I had has probably gone out the window now. So don't get all grateful, because I didn't do it for either of you. I did it for me. I've got my life to live. If anything happens to the big man who d'you think'll pay for it in the end?'

Leo phoned Macrae's house. The line was engaged. He sat for a moment, thinking, then he ran for his car.

21

'That's what I keep saying, Mum. It's on the cusp. That's right . . . With *what* in the ascendant? I dunno. It doesn't say.'

Frenchy was lying on Macrae's sofa, the phone to her ear. She was dressed in long leather boots, a miniskirt the size of a facecloth, and her favourite peek-a-boo top. Her hair fell about her face and she held a magazine in one hand. On her nose, and seemingly out of place, was a pair of spectacles. Frenchy was short-sighted.

'No, it says with the Sun in Aries it's good for affairs of the heart. Also good fortune . . . '

Macrae stood in the doorway looking at what was peek-ing and what was boo-ing. Normally he would have done something about Frenchy right there and then. But the tension of the past days had not only affected his stomach but also his libido. He hadn't been to bed with her in more than a week and he was getting looks with big question marks in them. He knew she was wondering if he was having it off with someone else. He wanted to say to her, 'Look, I'm having problems,' but could not find a way of doing it.

'No . . . No . . . Mum . . . You'll be all right. Why? Because it says so . . . ! Well, you order whatever paper you want, see what *it* says.'

She read from the magazine in her hands. ' "Good weather. Benign times." . . . Benign. Right. Means nothing bad.'

There was a quacking noise from the other end and Frenchy said, 'But that's in Africa or someplace. You don't get typhoons in Broadstairs in June.'

Macrae drew his finger across his throat. Frenchy nodded. 'Yeah . . . OK Mum. I'll ring you tomorrow.'

She put down the phone. 'Sorry, George. But you know what she's like. Typhoons, earthquakes. They worry her.'

'You've been talking for nearly an hour.'

'Well,' she said, with exasperating logic, 'you weren't using it.' That was undeniable but it irritated him.

'I might have wanted to.'

'Did you?'

'No, but someone might have wanted to ring me.'

'You're on holiday. Anyway, they'll ring back.'

'Next time you call your mother use your own phone.'

She gave him a hard look but said nothing. Instead she began to hum. It was a tuneless noise and she knew it drove Macrae out of his skull.

She got off the sofa and began to tidy up. She did it as a kind of knee-jerk reaction in Macrae's house; putting bottles and empty cigar packets into wastepaper baskets, folding bits of clothing . . .

He watched her with increasing irritation.

She went to the windows and looked out.

Hum . . . hum . . . hum . . . She swayed her bottom at him . . .

It was mid-afternoon but in the fog the light had gone and it was almost dark.

'Your street's looking up, George. You got some posh cars here now.'

She closed the curtains, put on the lights and went on with her tidying. She retrieved a piece of paper that had fallen down beside the telephone table.

'You want this, George?'

'What is it?'

'Can't make out the—Who's Gladys?'

'Let me have a look at it.'

It said, in an untidy scribble, 'Gladys. See housing man.'

He suddenly remembered Gladys' distressed call.

'I've got to go out,' he said.

'What?'

'See someone.'

'George, you said you had the whole day.'

'This won't take long. Just to Lambeth and back.'

174

She stood in front of him, arms akimbo. 'Tell me! Who're you going to see? Who is this Gladys?'

Macrae exploded. 'What bloody business is it of yours who I go to see?'

'You never told me about a Gladys?'

'Because there's nothing to tell!'

'Like you never told me about that Linda! You been seeing her!'

'So what if I have. She was my first wife. We've got things in common, a daughter for instance. Things to talk about.'

'It's rotten! Horrible! You say you love me and you're round there putting a leg over. It's not right!'

She began to cry.

'Oh, Jesus. Listen, stop your greetin'!'

'You said we were going out to dinner!' It was a wail.

'And we are. This won't take long.'

'George, don't go.' She hung on to his jacket.

'You have a bath,' he said, loosening her fingers. 'Work out your stars.'

He put on his coat and hat and went out into the fog.

Stoker, sitting in the Mercedes forty yards up the road, watched the big man come through the oblong of light as he opened and closed his front door. He started the engine. He waited for Macrae to come slightly nearer. He gunned the engine.

Two or three seconds and it would be over.

A lorry came slowly down the road, got between him and Macrae, and by the time it passed Macrae was inside his own car and was easing it out into the traffic. All Stoker could do was follow.

It was the dog, you see. Would he mind? She was frightened of him.

Simba? But he wouldn't hurt her. Wouldn't hurt anyone unless he told him to.

It was silly, she knew, but she wouldn't feel comfortable. He could tie Simba to the railings just outside her door. He'd be quite safe there. Or leave him in the car. It wouldn't be for long. It was only a leaky tap.

175

He didn't like it. That was plain enough. But he made the dog lie down outside the door.

Stay.

The dog stayed.

She let him in, pressed the door to behind her. Heard the lock click.

They were alone.

She'd bought these apples, she said. From the Cape of Good Hope. Really very good. Wouldn't he like one?

No, he didn't think so. He was looking at her oddly.

She was having one. A Granny Smith. Crisp. Full of juice.

He was sure they were lovely.

Here . . . she could cut him a piece.

No, really. Anyway he didn't like apples all that much.

She couldn't imagine that. Hadn't come across anyone who didn't like apples.

And she shouldn't be using that kind of knife, he said.

Why was that?

Carbon steel. It flavoured the fruit, and the acid in the apple would stain the blade. You wanted stainless steel for apples.

But stainless steel couldn't take an edge like carbon steel. That's what she'd been told anyway.

She was cutting fruit, he said, not flesh. What did she need carbon steel for?

How clever he was.

Tea? Coffee? A drink?

Nothing.

Nothing? Why was that?

Just didn't, that's all. Where was the leaking tap?

In the bathroom. Didn't he have tea or coffee or anything when Grace was here?

What did she mean?

Simple question.

What if he did? What if he didn't? What was it to her?

Life was full of questions. She had lots more. Especially about Grace.

Look – he had things to do – he didn't have much time—

Had he enjoyed himself?

Doing what?

176

Beating Grace up.

What was that supp—?

Like he'd beaten up the married woman.

He thought she'd better close her mouth.

Was that how he'd spoken to Grace? Is that how he spoke to women? His mother wouldn't have liked that. She'd have slapped his face for him.

Bitch!

Harold had called her that.

Had she been talking to him?

Of course she had. She'd been talking to him about Gerald. About his mind in particular. Was he crazy? Was he paranoid?

She was asking for it now.

Did he know Grace had written an entire account of their relationship? How he used to beat her up then cry and cry and be a little boy and want to suck her breasts? That was what he was all about wasn't it? A little boy looking for a mother to fuck. Someone to humiliate like he'd been humiliated.

If she wasn't careful he'd—

What? Beat her up too? He liked beating up women, didn't he? That's what turned him on wasn't it? And his dog, that was a sign too, wasn't it? And the Porsche? Was he angry? Was he bewildered? Didn't he realize yet that Grace was her daughter and that she had wanted to redeem him and that was what this was all about? Redemption. Did he know what redemption meant? She'd looked it up. It could mean salvation. It could also mean atonement.

Oh, and by the way, was he really an albino?

22

'Detective Superintendent Macrae,' said Macrae, and he held out his warrant card. 'You're the housing manager, aren't you? Mr Geach?'

'It's a fair cop, Inspector!' Geach was jovial.

Macrae saw a balding man in his thirties with what looked like a bad case of psoriasis of the scalp.

'Superintendent,' Macrae said.

'Sorry?'

'It's Detective Superintendent, not Inspector.'

'I stand corrected. What can I do you for, Superintendent? My old ladies been rioting again?'

Macrae sighed pensively. 'You a golfer, Mr Geach?'

The clubs stood against the wall in their brand-new bag. He picked out a seven-iron and tested it in his big hands. 'Expensive,' he said. 'What d'you play off?'

'Twenty-three.' A look of contempt crossed Macrae's face. 'But my handicap's coming down. It was twenty-eight.'

Macrae slipped the club back into the bag.

'You the housing manager of the whole estate, are you?'

'That's right. Is something wrong?'

'Wrong?' Macrae took off his hat and slumped in one of the chairs. 'Depends what you mean by wrong.'

'Well, you know we've got all sorts here. I mean there's drugs, sure, but it's no worse than a lot of estates. And some joy riding. But that's much better now that we've changed the pattern of the roads and put down "sleeping policemen". Kids mainly. They got nothing to do, no jobs. It's boredom really.'

'I haven't come about the kids, well, not in a direct sense. I've come about administration costs.'

A sudden wary look came into Geach's eyes.

'What're those, Inspector?'

Nothing irritated Macrae more than people calling him Inspector.

'That's what I was going to ask you about, Mr Geach.'

'Sorry. Can't help you there.'

'Oh. That's a pity. I thought you could. Administration costs and stamp duty.'

'Stamp duty? That's when you buy a house, isn't it? I mean we haven't sold the flats on this estate. No call for stamp duty.'

'That's what I thought. But . . . well, I have a problem, Mr Geach. There's someone on the estate, let's just call her an old friend. A widow. Used to be married to my driver in the police. And she's been worried by these yobs who haven't work to go to and who get bored. Just like you say. And they keep her awake at night wth their music and noise. You with me so far?'

'I'm with you, Inspector.'

'Just call me Mr Macrae if your memory's faulty.'

'What? Oh . . . sorry.'

'That's all right, laddie. I'm used to it. But to get back to what I was saying. These young louts keep my friend awake at night. And then she telephones me. Keeps me awake. You follow?'

'I follow. But what's all this got to do with me? I can't control them. Not even the police can't do that.'

'Well, now, she says she asked you for a transfer and—'

'Oh, yes. I remember her. Triffield, wasn't it? Mrs Triffield.'

'Twyford.'

'Of course. Twyford. Rosemary.' He made a thing of sorting through papers on his desk. 'Her application's here somewhere.'

'Don't fuss yourself. I believe you.'

'If you've come about trying to get her moved up the list then I'm sorry to say that everyone must take their proper turn unless it's socially desirable that they move or their health is at risk if they stay.'

'You didn't let me finish my wee story,' Macrae said patiently. 'You see this widow has a friend in high places.'

'Oh?' The eyes looked surprised. 'Who would that be?'

'Me. As far as you're concerned, Mr Geach, I'm the top of the mountain. The Himalayas. From where I stand you're just a wee pimple. You follow me?'

Geach did not reply.

'So we come to the administration costs and the stamp duty.'

'But I said—'

'Never mind a moment what you said. Just you listen to what I'm saying. Gladys – that's her name by the way – tells me you want five hundred quid for what you call administration costs and another fifty for stamp duty.'

Geach leaned back in his chair. 'Yeah. I remember her all right. Nutty as a fruit cake. Bats. Lost her marbles. She's been in twice or three times.' He leaned forward confidentially. 'I could have got her into serious trouble, Mr Macrae.'

'How's that?'

'Trying to bribe a council official.'

'Who would that be, Mr Geach?'

'Me. Tried to offer me money to move her to Briar.'

'Well now . . . How much did she offer you?'

'Four hundred, five hundred, something like that. I can't really remember. Happens all the time. People want to move. Pastures new. But there are lists, Mr Macrae. Hundreds and hundreds of families on the lists. It wouldn't be fair, would it? I mean we don't do business like that in England, do we?'

'I wouldn't know. I'm not English.'

'Well, you have my word that we don't.'

'And she got all this about administration costs and stamp duty . . . she got all that wrong?'

'She certainly did. You see what I mean. Dotty.'

Macrae rose. 'Well, thank you for your time, Mr Geach.'

'Not at all.' Geach rose with him. 'Glad to be of help.'

Macrae put on his hat and made for the door. Then stopped and turned. 'There's one thing that bothers me.'

'What's that?'

'You say she's senile.'

'Yeah . . . probably. A lot of them get like that here.'

'Aye. I've seen the place. It's no wonder. If you weren't mad before you came here you soon would be.'

'I wouldn't go so far as to say that.'

'The point I'm trying to make, Mr Geach, is that I saw her only a few weeks ago and she wasn't senile then. I didn't realize it came on so fast.'

180

'Well, maybe not senile. But you know . . . not all there. Anyway she tried to bribe me. No two ways aboout that.'

'All right then, I'll drop in and see her. Tell her I've discussed things with you and—'

'That's the best thing to do.'

'And then I'll go to one or two of the other houses – Briar, is it? – and I'll knock on some doors and have a wee talk to some of the older folk about how they got there and administration costs and stamp duty and then I'll come back here and ask for your records – and just clear the whole thing up to my satisfaction. You wouldn't mind that would you?'

Mr Geach had gone the colour of milk.

'Should I do that, Mr Geach?'

'Mr Macrae . . . Sir . . . I . . .'

'Sit down, Mr Geach, and let's talk about it man to man.'

Less than three hundred yards from Geach's office Gladys lay in her bed, terrified. First there had been ringing, then the banging. Was it on her door? Or the next flat's? Were they smashing down the barricades to get at her?

'Oh God,' she said to bulldog. 'What am I to do?'

The banging stopped.

'If I call the police and they come and there's no one here they won't come again. Cry wolf, they'll say.'

She lay stiffly on her back, all her old senses alert, but the banging did not start again.

Linda Macrae had had a frustrating time in more ways than one. As she sat in the taxi crossing the Thames on its way to Clapham she reviewed the past forty-eight hours without enthusiasm.

She tried to think of all the plusses. She now knew much more about the architecture and interior design of two of the world's busiest airports, Heathrow and Gatwick, than she had before.

That was a plus.

And she had become familiar, or at least as familiar as one could in dense fog, with the M25 motorway.

Was that a plus?

She had shuttled backwards and forwards between the two

airports as the fog lifted at one and closed down at the other.

She had been able to make certain judgements. Gatwick's coffee was better than Heathrow's; vice versa for the tea.

Interesting as these pieces of life's jigsaw were, they didn't come anywhere near being ravished. And being ravished – or something akin to it – was what she had set out to be, had planned to be, had looked forward to being.

Not only had she not been ravished, she had not even been chastely kissed by her would-be lover.

She hadn't even clapped eyes on him.

Memo to CEO British Airways. Subject: The sexual drive of divorced ladies in dense fog.

Neither she nor David had missed the irony. She had phoned him from Heathrow. By that time she had already got as far north as Manchester, only to be turned back to London.

'David, it is not meant to be,' she had said.

'It's completely clear here.'

'Where's here?'

'Loch Inver.'

'Where's that?'

'Near the top of Scotland on the left-hand side.'

'Is there an international airport there?'

'Let me look out of the hotel window . . . No . . . Not that I can see. There's a football pitch. Glider?'

'I'm going home.'

Which is what she'd done.

She paid off the cab and slung her flight bag over her shoulder and was walking up the path from the gate when she heard the dog. In the foggy darkness close at hand came a long-drawn-out howl. It was a sound from the *taiga* and it froze her blood.

She stopped. She could hear whining, then the howl came again. It was coming from the bottom of the basement steps that led down to Irene's flat.

'Good dog,' she said.

There was an ominous, grating growl.

She had no torch so she unlocked the front door and switched on the porch light. Now she could see the basement steps and Irene's front door. A huge brown dog stood on the doormat. It gave another chilling howl and then began to scratch wildly at the door. Chips and splinters of wood had already been scraped away and parts of the architrave had been bitten.

There was something familiar about the dog.

'Simba. Good Simba.'

The dog howled.

If Gerald was there why wasn't he responding? He and the dog were inseparable. She stepped across a small lawn and saw that there was light in Irene's sitting-room windows. But the curtains were closed.

Perhaps Gerald had come round for some reason. Perhaps he had taken Irene for a drink.

She went back into the street and looked at the cars. She walked about thirty yards before she saw the Porsche. She didn't understand what was going on but decided she must get indoors. She could phone the police or the fire brigade or whoever it was who looked after intransigent animals.

She began to walk back to her house and as she did so she heard a footstep, just the scraping of a leather shoe on concrete. She paused but the sound was not repeated.

She hurried forward. The heavy air smelled of exhaust fumes and she could not see more than twenty yards.

She heard the footsteps once more.

For God's sake, she told herself, it was early evening; people were coming home from work. It would have been surprising if she *hadn't* heard footsteps.

She walked up her path. He was waiting for her in the front garden. A dark shape in the dark mist. She turned and began to run. He was on top of her in a flash.

'Linda!'

'Oh God, Leo! You scared me to death!'

'Sorry about that. I was looking for my guv'nor.'

'George? Well, he's not here. Why would you think that?'

'His . . . the girl . . . I was told at his house he might be here or at Gladys Twyford's place. I've been there. But he's not.'

'I've only just got back from—'

The dog howled and scratched.

'What on earth's that? Sounds like the Hound of the Baskervilles.'

'It's the estate agent's dog. Leo, I think something's wrong.'

183

23

Macrae felt slightly cheered. Interviews with people like Geach often cheered him. Now he was the bearer of good tidings which was something that didn't often happen to him. He could ring Gladys that evening or the following day or he could go and tell her now. He decided to play Father Christmas and set off on foot along the road that led to Rosemary House.

Where they came from he never knew. One moment he was plodding along the curving road, the next, like fetches, they were simply there, ghostly shapes in the mist. They stopped, stood on the muddy grass at the side of the road and, incredibly at first, seemed about to let him pass.

Macrae was afraid. He wasn't often afraid, but he was now.

No eye contact, he told himself.

He had read somewhere that in Africa predators always killed the animal that broke and ran. He did not change his pace. He was almost past the group of youths when one shouted. 'I know 'im. He's a fuckin' copper.'

Only a few words, but a war cry.

They came at him from all sides and Macrae's fleeting memory of Africa was not far-fetched. The youths were like Cape hunting dogs attacking an isolated buffalo. They came from behind – he felt blows on his legs – and from the sides. He saw a half-brick, he saw a bicycle chain, he saw a length of metal tubing.

Don't fall! Don't fall!

Under the orange sodium lights which gave the fog an unearthly colour, he fought back. It was unscientific, uneducated. He swung punches, sometimes connecting, sometimes not. He grabbed hair, ears, anything he could lay his hands on. But there were too many of them. They hit and kicked, their hard Doc Martens thudded into his calves and thighs. One jumped on to his back and pressed an iron bar against his throat.

It was then he knew they were going to kill him. They might not mean to kill him but they were in the grip of a mob hysteria that was communicating itself, from one to the next, like a frenzy.

Don't fall!

But he could not stand. His legs were being battered and kicked, his strength was going. They pushed him, he staggered, his foot hit one of Geach's 'sleeping policemen' – and he went down.

The pack was on him in an instant. He pulled up his legs into the foetal position to protect his genitals and his stomach and covered what he could of his head and face with his arms and hands.

It was all he could do.

So far, the youths had preserved a grim silence while they beat him. Now he heard a voice he recognized.

'Here! Give us a go!'

Through his fingers he could see Stoker. He had a tyre lever in his hand.

'My turn!'

Stoker grabbed one of the youths and pulled him aside to get at Macrae. The youth was far gone in a state of savage hysteria and the interruption was like igniting an additional emotional fuse.

A blow, meant for Macrae, changed its parabolic arc and found Stoker's kneecap.

'Christ!' he yelled.

Someone swung a chain and caught him in the mouth. Blood flowed on to his chin.

'Don't!' he shouted. 'I hates coppers. I'm one of you!'

One of them? For an instant they stopped as they digested this unlikely statement.

Stoker picked a tooth from his mouth and stared dully at it.

'Look what you did!' he said.

Then he turned and ran.

They were after him in a flash. A moving target.

Macrae heard the unmistakable sounds of flesh and bone being pounded. He heard a cry. Then he crawled away. He pulled himself along on his elbows like some stricken saurian.

Great mountains reared above him. A line of dustbins. He crawled behind them and lay unconscious for the better part of twenty minutes.

Slowly his senses returned. He began to test the exposed parts of his body, then the extremities. Nothing broken. His heavy coat had saved him. But he was bleeding from the mouth and nose.

At his feet was a bundle of newspapers neatly tied for the dustmen to remove. He sat up, ripped up a newspaper and cleaned his face and hands. Slowly he rose to his feet. He was shaky and dizzy. He knew his car was only fifty yards away. But could he make it?

He lifted the lid of a dustbin to throw away the blood-stained paper. In the light from the nearest sodium lamp he found himself looking down at Stoker. He had been stuffed into the bin in a sitting position. For a moment Macrae thought he was alive. Then he looked into the staring eyes and realized they would never see anything again.

Carefully he lowered the lid, put the newspaper into his coat, and, keeping to the grass, silently made his way back to his car.

Leo Silver and Linda Macrae stood on Irene's terrace.

They had phoned the estate agency from Linda's flat but only got an answering machine. Leo was anxious to be off in search of Macrae and did not want to become embroiled in something that wasn't in his patch.

But Linda had been firm. 'We can't just leave things,' she said. As she spoke the dog howled again. 'We must check that she's all right.'

They had banged on windows and doors, carefully avoiding the dog, but there had been no reply.

And so they had come to the terrace and Leo was looking at the french doors. 'I'll have to break the glass,' he said.

'I thought the police could pick locks. George always said—'

'The key's in the lock on the other side.'

He took a brick from the garden and carefully smashed a single pane next to the door handle. He put in his hand, turned the key, opened the door, pushed the heavy curtains aside – and they were in.

The room was warm and well lit. Cosy. As though it was expecting company.

'Irene!' Linda called.

The dog answered with hysterical barking.

'What's that?' Linda said, looking at something that had fallen partly under a chair.

Leo bent and picked it up. 'Apple,' he said. 'She must have been eating—'

He stopped. The juice of this grass-green apple was stained with red. 'Oh, Jesus!' he said.

The trail of blood led across the carpet. They followed it into Irene's bedroom.

The two bodies were interlocked on the floor. The man's body with the knife deep in his stomach lay on top, the woman, her face purple and her eyes bulging out of their bloody sockets, underneath. His dead fingers still lay at her throat.

24

It was a bright, brisk morning. The fog had gone and the sun was out.

Macrae lay in his bed. Frenchy had decided to give him a breakfast she considered would help return him to the man he had been. There was bacon, eggs, sausages, a steak, fried bread, grilled tomatoes, and chips.

Macrae, sore and battered, looked at this in apprehension and dismay.

'Lassie, I'll never—'

'Just get your teeth around this, George, and you'll feel a lot better. I'm going to have a bath then I'm coming to dress your cuts.'

'Cuts' was a general understatement for the bruises, contusions, abrasions, wounds, and general havoc which had been done to his body.

'And then I'm going to give you a sponge bath.'

He was too weak to argue.

When he had got back from Lambeth she had been appalled by what she had seen; so much so that she had phoned Rambo and told him she would not be working until further notice and was threatening to ring certain other numbers which would bring down vengeance on the yobs. Macrae had asked her to desist and from then on she had been a regular little Florence Nightingale.

He heard the water run into her bath. Slowly and painfully he levered himself out of bed, found a plastic shopping bag, emptied the plate of food into it, and hid it on the top of his wardrobe.

He crawled back into bed, drank his coffee, and lit a cigar. He was supposed to return to work the following day but had extended his leave by a week.

He wondered what Scales would say. He wondered if he had even the slightest inkling of what had been going on. No . . . Scales was too much a bloody desk-wallah to have pipelines into the underworld. And even if he did know, Stoker was dead and he was sure Molly would never come after him on her own.

He wondered if he should see her; do something about the tapes. Probably be a good idea.

Some time.

He had never thought he'd be grateful to a bunch of hooligans. But he was. He'd assumed they were all in their late teens but the local community copper who'd gone into the estate and pulled them in had told Macrae that one of them was only twelve. God knew what that little darling would be like when he grew up; another Stoker perhaps.

Which reminded him, he'd have to phone Norman Paston and tell him there was nothing to the rumour about the bent copper. He'd enjoy that.

And then there was Silver. What the hell did he know? It was apparent that he knew something. Didn't matter at the moment. They'd sort it out.

The point was, nothing mattered at the moment. There was just the pain and his cigar.

His mind went back over several incidents. Buckle . . . Gladys (she'd be all right now) . . . Irene what'shername . . .

Silver had told him the details. 'The strange thing was the apples,' he'd said. 'She was crazy about apples. They were everywhere. She had a bowl in the sitting-room, one in her bedroom. Even one in the bathroom. Some of them half-eaten.'

Macrae's mind had been ticking over as he listened, now it went into gear. 'And knives?' he said.

'Oh, sure. You know, the sort cooks use. She used one on the estate agent. Must have grabbed it when he came for her. I mean she was nearly bloody lucky, guv'nor.'

'Aye. Nearly.'

He realized he had unwittingly outlined to Irene a *modus operandi* for murder by self-defence. He felt a momentary convulsion of conscience. But what the hell, people who were going to commit murder usually did. And remembering her eyes he realized that nothing he might have said or left unsaid would have changed it. Only the method.

Frenchy came back from her bath and saw the empty plate. 'That's good, George. You must be feeling better.'

'It's your cooking,' he said, gallantly.

'Well, you have a sleep, and I'll have a little peruse downstairs.'

She picked up *Our Mutual Friend*; all nine hundred paperback pages.

'You're sure you want that?' he said.

'You like it, so I'll like it. Anyway, I like reading about people's friends.'

Less than a couple of miles from Macrae's house, Leo and Zoe were also in bed. They had just finished making love and Leo was still lying on top of her, his bones turned to rubber, fighting the desire to drift off into sleep.

She patted his naked bottom. 'That was very nice indeed,' she said. 'Leopold Silver – Lover.'

'Uuuuuuuuuuuuhhhhhh,' he said, and rolled on to his own side of the bed.

After a while she said, 'Leo? Are you asleep?'

'Uuuuuuuuuhhhh.'

'What's going to happen now with this Macrae thing?'

'Scales is going to go ape. That's what's going to happen. No Stoker, no debt; no debt, no stick to beat Macrae with.'

'I thought you were brilliant. I would have told you except it would have given you a swollen head.'

'Thanks. Listen, what about going out for lunch? What about driving out into the country? Something like that.'

She raised herself on her elbow and looked down at him. 'Do you know what day this is? This is the day all good boys eat with their parents.'

'I'll ring my mother.'

'God, Leo, what'll you say?'

'I'll lie.'

'Wow. And then we can come back to bed this afternoon and do this all over again.'

'Uuuuuuuuhhhh!'

'But only if you feel strong enough.'

He lay back and looked at the ceiling. He felt tired but happy. 'What's that?' he said.

'What's what?'

'On the ceiling.'

It was one of the signs she had lettered to welcome him back.

' "Home is the hunter",' he read. 'You've got it wrong.'

'I've got it what?'

'It doesn't go like that.'

'My God! Leo, you're getting impossible!'

'Well, it doesn't. It goes—'

'I'm waiting.'

'Listen, it's one of the most misquoted lines in the world.'

'OK, well, quote it correctly then.'

'It goes . . . Oh, Christ, I can't remember exactly how it goes. But take my word for it.'

'No, Leo, I will not take your word for it. Where's our book of quotations?'

'Upstairs.'

Naked, she got out of bed and ran across the room.

Leo turned to the wall. He might just be able to get a couple of minutes' sleep before she came back.

Molly Gorman walked along the paths of one of those bleak cemeteries that spread for miles beside the Southern Railway. Finally she came to Stoker's grave. The earth was fresh, which distinguished it from its neighbours. One day she might order a headstone for it. She hadn't known whether he wanted to be cremated or buried so she'd had to make the decision.

It was a pity about Gary. But it wouldn't have lasted. Funny, she must have seen him around as a little boy without even knowing who he was. Now he was gone.

First the father, then Gary, but what else could she have done? It was everyone for themselves in this life and once the old bill got their hooks into you, they never let go.

191

She felt sad. Cemeteries always made her feel sad. She didn't think she'd come again.

She placed a wreath of plastic flowers on the grave and began the long walk back to her car.

They were selling forced daffodils at the cemetery gates; the first signs of spring.

Thank God January was over.